SO TO HONOR HIM

THE MAGI AND THE DRUMMER

LAURA VANARENDONK BAUGH

Æclipse Press
Indianapolis, IN

First paperback and electronic editions published 2014.
Second paperback and electronic editions published 2015.

DEDICATION

Inasmuch as many have undertaken to compile an account of the things accomplished among us, just as they were handed down to us by those who from the beginning were eyewitnesses and servants of the word, it seemed fitting for me as well, having investigated everything carefully from the beginning, to write it out for you in consecutive order, most excellent Theophilus; so that you may know the exact truth about the things you have been taught.

For all the eyewitnesses and servants,
and for all seekers, everywhere.

CHAPTER ONE

"BUT he plays a woman's instrument," the tall man observed, his dark eyes faintly disgusted. "How useful could he be?"

Arash did not look up. They would not want to see his eyes, would not want to see anything that tasted of defiance. He needed to appear obedient, quiet, compliant. He could not afford to displease this customer too.

He had not gotten a good look at this man, but that hardly mattered. It was not his place to evaluate his future master, but rather to be evaluated. And while Hooshman had erred in advertising this particular young slave's unconventional musicianship, he would hold it Arash's fault for failing to meet his customers' heightened expectations.

"I believe he had the learning of it from his mother," Hooshman said. "You cannot expect that slaves would know the right of things. But he is passing fair at it."

The tall man shook his head. "No, I don't want to pay the higher price for a musician when he can't even play for my guests. I'd look foolish with a boy playing. No, show me something else."

Hooshman's mouth tightened and he waved Arash away. "No matter," he said, "no matter, there are plenty of others."

Arash heard the restrained note of frustration and winced inwardly, knowing Hooshman would find some blame in him for this lost sale. Fingers tight around his skin drum, Arash bent low and started back toward the door, the metal shackle chafing his ankle.

Before he reached it, another voice spoke. "I'd like to hear the boy play."

Arash stopped and waited, his eyes on the floor. Hooshman turned. "Forgive me, good sir! I did not see you enter. You wish to hear him?"

"It's hard to judge the worth of a musician without hearing his music," the second customer said reasonably. "But I will wait, if you wish to finish with this gentleman first."

Arash could imagine Hooshman's consternation, caught between two customers. "Why wait?" he said quickly. "The boy may play for you while I take this gentleman on to see other stock. If that pleases you?"

"It does." Arash heard the creak of a chair settling under weight. "Please."

Hooshman snapped his fingers. "Go and play, boy." Arash heard the unspoken threat: *Acquit yourself well. Sell yourself. Do not disappoint.*

Arash went to the newcomer and knelt on the floor, cradling his drum. "What would it please my lord to hear?" he asked, his eyes on the man's feet. They were wealthy feet, well-tended and clean.

"Play what you like," the man said. "Whatever you think shows your skill."

Arash nodded once, drawing a slow breath. He did not like the onus placed upon him; it was easier to fulfill an order than to anticipate a desire. But the man seemed to be interested in a drummer, and so Arash would show him his best drumming.

He set the drum firmly in his support hand, exhaled in a long stream to steady his fingers, and began to play.

He started with a brisk rhythm, a syncopated series calling both high and low tones from the skin drum. Then he began to slap the drum over the continuing rhythm. Sharp metallic notes leapt above the throbbing bass called from the center of the skin. His fingers leapt upon the surface, tapping and brushing and stroking, and he introduced a quick

rolling sequence that made his fingers flash too quickly
to be seen. He rocked slightly with the music, his own
pulse lost in the beat of the drum.

He pressed the rhythm faster, driving to a
crescendo, and then let it crash into quiet, a mere
heartbeat of sound which ran on for a half-dozen
breaths, and then he finished with a flourish and a final
deep-toned slap.

The silence was oppressive, and Arash hardly
dared to breathe. The music had shown a number of
techniques, it had been by turns both energetic and
soulful, and surely, *surely* this interested stranger
would care to hear more?

"He's not what I expected," came a comment
from across the room. The first man had paused in the
doorway, rather than following Hooshman on to look
over the other slaves. Arash, still looking at the
newcomer's feet, could see peripherally the first man
half-turning to Hooshman behind him. "I may take
him after all. What are you asking for him?"

"With the greatest of respect," said the second
man, "I believe I have the greater claim, as it was I who
asked after him only after you had passed him over."

Arash's stomach writhed within him. He could
almost hear Hooshman's grin — with two customers
interested in the slave, it might be possible to drive up
the price, and there would be no chastisement for

failing to present himself well. Yet there was always fear with any sale, going to a new master.

Arash swallowed, waiting to hear the debate over who would take possession of him. But the first customer gave a small sniff and said, "Well, then, as you wish. It's nothing to me; he's only a novelty." And then he turned out, so that Hooshman had to hurry after him.

Arash sat still, wondering if the man who had been interested to hear a slave boy play would be a kind master, or at least a fair one.

"Raise your face, boy, and let me see you."

Arash lifted his chin, but kept his eyes lowered.

The man sighed. "Look at me, then."

Arash did, able to freely observe him for the first time. The man wore Persian garb, a belted tunic and many-folded trousers, of rich fabric but practical. His beard was short and neatly trimmed, and his mustache nearly obscured his mouth. He observed Arash for a moment. "Were you always a slave, boy, or were you sold for debt or some other cause?"

"I was born a slave, master, in the Roman territory."

The man nodded. Slavery was uncommon in Persian culture, and Arash might have as easily been a freeman. But he had been born in Roman territory, the child of a slave, and so Hooshman, a Persian who traded between his own country and the Roman cities, was free to sell him as he might a table or donkey.

"Roman territory? Do you speak anything besides Persian, then?"

"I was raised to speak Greek. And," Arash hurried to offer, "a little Aramaic, from Idumean slaves in the household."

"Well, that will be useful. What's your name?"

"Arash, master, if it pleases you."

"It does please me, Arash, as did your music. Could you play for a company on a journey, to keep them content when the comforts of home are left long behind?"

"Of course, master."

He nodded. "Then I shall buy you of Hooshman. It will be a long road yet, but in the end there's much to like about Tyspwn."

Arash caught his breath. Tyspwn was the capital of Parthia. He had not dreamed of returning to the heart of his mother's country. And if his new master took him to a land where slavery was rare, might it be… could it come to pass that he might be granted his freedom? Could he earn it more rapidly in such a place?

He nodded obediently and dropped his eyes again. It would not do to display such hope openly, especially not here while yet in Hooshman's house. There was time enough to discover what lay ahead.

Arash's new master was called both Saman and Marcus Corvidus, as he was Persian nobility by birth and a citizen of Rome by his own accomplishment. This seemed to lie somehow in a service he had once rendered a senator. More, Saman was one of the Megistanes.

Arash had heard his Persian mother speak a little of the Megistanes, but he remembered only that they were hereditary priests and ministers of the court. They were supposed to be great scholars, he thought, the wisest of men.

Within a few minutes of their arrival at the inn, Saman had consigned Arash to a tall Greek with orders to turn Arash over to someone called Tannaz, and then he disappeared to other rooms, trailed by another servant with a sheaf of papers and tablets. For half an hour Arash sat in the yard, waiting for Tannaz, and listened to the inn's guests and servants gossip.

Tannaz turned out to be the Megistanes' chief steward, a dark-skinned man who immediately accused Arash of fleas and sent him to bathe. Arash, who did not have fleas, did not argue. It was unwise to present a first impression of recalcitrance. Once identified as troublesome, all a slave's actions were viewed through a veil of prejudice.

The slaves' bath was clean and serviceable, if lacking in ornamentation. Arash unclasped his arms from about the frame drum he had held close all the while and set it to one side.

Carrying the drum into the bath might affect its voice, as the skin would absorb some of the humidity of the room, but Arash had nowhere to leave it outside and would not be separated from it, anyway. Slaves could own property, in many cases, but Arash had only the drum and his own skin. The drum had been his mother's. It was about the length of his forearm, a simple frame of wood with goat skin stretched across it. It bore no decoration. She had taught him to play as she did, even though he was a son, and often she had sung to accompany his drum — until he had been sold away to the city of Philadelphia, six years ago.

He placed the drum on a low bench and shed his clothes. Despite his resentment of Tannaz's allegation, the water did look inviting.

He sluiced water over himself and then ducked his head, soaking his dark, waving hair and scrubbing himself clean of dust, dry skin, and any fleas which might somehow have leapt on him between Hooshman's and the bath. He took a few extra minutes to stretch and rub his limbs in the warm water, enjoying the time to himself; privacy and introspection had been rare in Hooshman's mercantile care. Then he rose, toweled himself, and began to dress in the new clothes which had been sent to the baths with him. Probably Tannaz had distrusted his clothing, too.

He turned back to the bench where he had left his drum, but it was empty. He glanced from side to side, but it had not fallen to the floor — as if it somehow could have, after Arash left it safely flat.

Arash's stomach tightened and twisted, and he spun in place, looking vainly about the small bath. That drum was his only possession, his best memory of his mother, and the sole barrier between Arash's sale as a musician and his sale as a sweeper of camel dung. And it was gone.

A chuckle escaped over a low wall, and someone laughingly shh'd the laugher. Arash bolted for the door and swung with one hand on the frame to face three teen boys, who turned to face him. "Give it back!" Arash demanded.

The crouching boys rose and fanned slightly so that they flanked Arash against the wall. Two were taller than he and the third was broader. "Give back what?" the broad one asked.

Arash looked at each of them. "Give it back," he repeated. "My drum."

"Your drum?" repeated a tall one. He had blond hair and a lean, muscular build. "Why would you have a drum?"

"My master purchased me for a drummer." Arash wanted his voice to be even and firm, but it wavered even to his ears. "I must have it or be found delinquent." He wished he knew if these boys were slaves to the same master Saman, and thus could be threatened, or subject to some other man and therefore immune from any threats Arash might make. Or they might even be freemen, wholly untouchable unless Arash could bring a reasonable argument to a new master who had no reason to believe an unknown slave over the word of freemen.

"Your master will be disappointed in you, then," said the other tall one. He had straight brown hair which needed cutting. "Because I haven't seen any drums around here." He looked at the broad one. "Have you seen any drums around here?"

They laughed.

Despair began to throb in Arash's chest. "Please," he tried, "just return it to me. I'll say nothing. Only give it back."

"Look how quickly he begs!" the brown-haired one jeered.

"Give what back?" repeated the broad one. He was unoriginal, Arash noted, but that made him no less problematic.

"Unless you mean the drum in the pool outside?" The blond grinned.

Arash's heart seized for an instant, and then he bolted half-dressed into the yard. He raced through the yard to the little pool where the beasts of burden were watered. It wasn't far, as it shared a water line with the baths. A little fountain supplied it from the channel, and there on the corner of the sluice hung the drum, one edge of its round frame hooked tenuously over the edge of the waterway. It rotated slightly as occasionally splashes of water reached it and spun it on its point of balance.

Arash climbed onto the edge of the pool and stretched out his arm, but his fingertips could not reach the drum. He reached to rest a hand on the waterway to stretch further, but it moved with his weight and he jerked back.

Laughter came from behind him. "What's the matter?" pressed the broad one. "Haven't you found your drum? Aren't you happy now?"

Two of them must have hung it together, or one of them must have tossed it with great precision — or luck. But Arash couldn't drop it into the water now and risk its ruin. He bit fiercely on the inside of his lip, trying to think of a solution against the hooting laughter behind him.

"Jump for it!" called the blond. "Go on, jump!"

Arash had already seen it. If he could leap from the lip of the pool, he might snatch the drum before splashing down into the pool itself. He would have to shield it from the water, but it was his best hope if he were to retrieve it himself.

He ignored the mockery behind him and leapt, swinging his arms to extend his jump and reach as much as he could. His hand caught the lip of the frame and his fingers locked around it as he fell toward the shallow pool. His feet slid from beneath him and he fell backward into the water. Desperately he shoved the drum upward, trying to keep it above the surface as he went under.

Immediately he convulsed upward, coughing and spitting and trying to clear his eyes so he could see the drum. It was wet with droplets, but it had not gone under with him. It seemed to be otherwise unharmed.

The three boys were howling and clutching their stomachs with laughter. All about the yard, men and women were staring toward the fountain. Arash sloshed toward the edge of the pool and stepped dripping over the lip.

Despite the water streaming from his hair, his face and ears burned. "When I am free," he snarled, "you won't dare to treat me so."

He regretted the words as soon as they struck the air, hated putting his dearest desire in the view of these sadistic toughs. But there was no recalling them.

"Free?" The blond boy folded with fresh laughter. "When you are free!"

Arash clenched his fists. "If you ever touch my drum again—"

The broad boy tackled him from the side, and they tumbled across the yard, scraping limbs and banging elbows against stone. Arash did not strike at his assailant but folded protectively about his drum, pressing it close to his abdomen as the boys closed. Someone kicked him in the lower back, and someone else stomped his ribs. A spray of dirt spattered against his face.

"Hold, you ruffians!" It was Tannaz's voice, and Arash was grateful for the irritable steward. The boys drew back, and a trio of protesting voices began proclaiming their innocence and Arash's treachery.

Arash rubbed dirt from his eyes and sat up, his bruised ribs already protesting. Tannaz had caught the blond boy by the back of the neck and was glowering at the other two. "I suppose he left the bath half-naked then and came out alone to attack the three of you? Even a Persian brat can at least do that much math." He looked at Arash. "Get up. What was it, then?"

Arash pushed the back of his arm across his mouth to clear it of dirt but only made it worse. "My drum," he said. "They took my drum."

Tannaz's eyes nearly rolled with weary outrage. "That's the strap for you," he said to the broad boy, "and for you," to the brown-haired. "And cut your hair." He gave a little shake to the blond whose neck he gripped. "And I'll see you whipped. I've had enough of your disruptions and petty thieveries, and this was nearly destructive beside. If your master purchases a drummer and you immediately deprive him of the drum, how do you think your master will view it? You're lucky we're not making a replacement from your skin."

The blond continued his protestations, alternately pleading and threatening, but Tannaz was not impressed. He turned back to Arash. "Get up, I said." He scowled, running his eyes over Arash's muddied form. "I supposed you'll need to bathe fresh, then. And that must be the new clothing, of course." He sighed. "I'll have another set sent to the baths. Get back there before someone sees you and you disgrace the name of your master." He frowned, his eyes tracing the scarring over Arash's bare back. "Though it seems you're no stranger to trouble yourself."

"That was not how you think," Arash said quickly.

Tannaz shook his head. "I've no time for excuses now." He gave a sharp pinch to the blond boy's nape, drawing a fresh squeal and series of arguments, and started away with the boy in tow.

Arash went into the bath and sat on the bench, sponging the dust and water from the drum. It was unharmed, and the voice largely unchanged.

He wrapped it in a towel and set it against the wall, and when he entered the water he remained facing it, never taking his eyes from it.

Arash was seated against a wall, hugging the face of his drum to his chest to warm and dry it, when Tannaz found him.

"There you are!" Tannaz looked as irascible as ever, and more harried. "You're wanted in the hall, for the banquet. Everyone's arrived at last, and they'll be needing music when they've done making their introductions."

Arash nodded, ashamed under Tannaz's disapproving gaze and his quick inspection for any remaining mud. The steward found nothing to criticize, and Arash followed the stream of servants bearing trays of savory-smelling food toward the banqueting hall.

Great men were seated in the hall, reclining on cushions about the low tables. There were olives and figs and dates on the tables, but the men were talking more than eating. Arash hesitated behind a fountain and let his eyes search over them in quiet wonder. It was good to know something of the men his music would be expected to please.

There was a pale man with light-colored hair, who would be tall when he rose from the cushion. He had a prominent nose and chalky teeth. The men on either side of him were Parthian, olive-skinned and dark-haired. These must be other Megistanes, Arash supposed as he stared.

But there were others around the tables, and Arash scanned them from his place behind the fountain. All were well-dressed, men of obvious learning and standing. One man with narrow, upturned eyes knelt at the table, not reclining like the Parthians. He wore garments of silk — entirely of silk. Arash gaped freely from his concealment. The man might have dressed all in gold coins and displayed his wealth as plainly.

Beside this stranger sat several men dressed in brilliant white linen and ornamented with gold and ivory jewelry. Another man wore clothing very like the Greek style, but the language he spoke to the muslin-robed man beside him was one Arash had never heard. Arash had been raised in the Decapolis and was accustomed to all manner of coloring and dress and speech, but he had not seen men like these before. Why were they with his master and the Megistanes?

Then his master Saman was rising to his feet, and the room's conversation fell silent. Arash shrank behind the fountain, one hand on his drum to keep it silent.

"Gentlemen, learned scholars, colleagues," began Saman, "I have been granted the great privilege of welcoming each of you. Tonight our number is complete, with all arrived and assembled for the journey. Many of you are known to one another already, but not all. I should like to introduce each, so that we may be as one in unity and purpose."

He nodded to the pale man with chalky teeth. "Bithisarea, you are most welcome here. Melichior, and Gathaspa, your expertise is invaluable to our enterprise. Kagpha, Badadakharida, Badadilma, thank you for lending your wise experience and learning."

The men nodded and looked around with pleasant smiles.

"Gondophares, we are pleased to have you with us. Larvandad, Gushnasaph, Hormisdas, welcome, and I am sure we all hope our journey together leads only to greater cooperation between our sects. Hor, Karsudan, Basanater, I cannot express how grateful we are for such knowledgeable companions."

Men around the tables inclined their heads or lifted their hands in turn, nodding to their colleagues and smiling welcomes to one another.

"Cao He, we are truly honored by your dedication to travel so far and to seek us out."

The man in silks bowed from his waist. "The honor is mine, Saman. Our opportunity is unique."

"That is aptly spoken," agreed Gathaspa. "For centuries we have awaited this, long generations, and now we will see it fulfilled."

"We have scholars here from the great places of the world," said Gondophares. "It is not often that such an assembly may meet and travel together. Surely this new king must be marked by heaven."

"Dine well, friends," said Saman, "for tomorrow we continue westward toward Judea, to seek this new king and so to honor him with gifts. Let us begin our journey with joy." His eye caught Arash behind the fountain, and he gestured.

Arash came out and sat where his new master indicated. He began a lively but soft rhythm on the drum, something suitable to run beneath good conversation and wine.

Saman sat down with the others, and Arash watched him, hoping to learn something of the man who now determined his life. Saman was not the greatest among the gathered scholars, but he was respected, and even liked. That would have to do for a start.

But they were not going to Tyspwn, that much was clear. These great men had gathered from all the parts of the world for some journey together, and they would take Arash along with them to drum.

CHAPTER TWO

IT took hours to get underway the next morning. The inn, large and luxurious as it was, turned out to house only the Megistanes and scholars and their personal servants. The bulk of their company, including a thousand cavalry — Arash boggled at the mention of it — were encamped outside the city.

"A thousand mounted soldiers?" he repeated.

"Of course, and be glad of it," said Leandros. He was yet another of the seemingly endless entourage. Tannaz had told Arash to keep close to Leandros and help him however was needed. "These are great men, important men, and their word sways nations. They can't go unprotected among whatever rabble might be congregating in the scrub-lands. And then there are the gifts, you know. It's customary to bring gifts to a new king, and wouldn't the bandits love to take those? Judea's a fine place for bandits, though I hear King Herod has been winnowing them down. And of course there's King Herod himself, as I wouldn't care to suppose how he'll take to such men of state riding into his province. He's not exactly opened an alliance with the Parthian empire. Say, can't you put that drum down and use your hands properly? You're more than half useless like that. Pack it in somewhere."

Arash thought of the boys in the bath and courtyard. "Is there a bag or satchel I could wear and carry it?"

The spare bag Leandros found for him was the simplest of designs, a basic wrap of cloth with a long sling. Arash lay the strap over his shoulder and across his chest so that the drum, nestled in the bag, lay on the opposite hip.

At last all was assembled, loaded onto or behind donkeys, camels, horses, and oxen. The train was impressively long, certainly the largest Arash had seen in his limited experience. As they wound out of the city, they seemed to stretch across the countryside, preceded and followed and flanked by the mounted soldiers.

"Has anyone told you yet about the star?" Leandros plainly hoped no one had.

Arash obliged him. It was good to make friends where he could, particularly if the boys who had stolen his drum might be somewhere in the long caravan. And anyway, he didn't know about it. "What star?"

"You haven't heard about the star?" Leandros feigned indignant surprise over his obvious pleasure. "It's the reason we're here. The Megistanes saw it back in the east, rising out of Judea it seemed, and it burned like no ordinary star. This was a star for the birth of a king, and a mighty king indeed. And so they conferred among themselves and determined that this star told the birth of a new king of the Jews."

Arash frowned. "Why would the Megistanes care for the Jews' king?"

"Watch that grain sack! Tie the mouth again, that's better. Well, plainly this king is to be something more than King Herod. Not that outshining Herod would be difficult, mind you — he's only half-Jewish, and his father's an Idumean anyway, so he's hardly one of them. And he's a panting spaniel to the Romans, that's plain to see. And for all he builds his temples and walls and fortresses, his own people hate him, so that has to say something. They say he has secret night-men who inform on malcontents or anyone speaking against him, and do dark retribution to anyone Herod deems dangerous." Leandros nodded conspiratorially. "I knew a Jew who was slave to my previous master, and his whole family was seized and sold by Herod's father to help pay for some

Roman war. He set me straight about Herod, you see."

"I see."

"Your drum's dangling, there. Might want to shift that bag back behind you if you're going to wear it all the time."

Arash pushed the bag with his drum behind his hip. "What do you know of Saman?"

"Saman? Is that the one who's your new master?"

Arash nodded.

"Can't say I know too much about him personally," said Leandros. "Grab the lead for that donkey and tug him back this way, see the one? He's not fond of the camels, likes to drift away from them, but we like to keep the line orderly. No, I'm with Basanater, and he's a decent enough fellow. Sits up with his star charts, mostly."

Arash chose his next words carefully. "There's not many slaves in the Parthian lands, isn't that so?"

"What? No, I'm no slave, that's certain. I sell my service for a fair price, and Basanater is happy to pay it. But Saman's a Roman as well as a Parthian, and I suppose he has a few Roman habits. I think the senator who gave him his citizenship also gave him slaves, though I don't know what became of them all. But Tannaz manages everyone well enough, slave and free servant — even the Seres servants who came from the land of silk, which is quite a feat, as they don't speak anything I can make out myself."

"Tell me about the senator," Arash said. "How did Saman receive his citizenship?"

"I don't know all the details. This was a dozen years ago, maybe. I don't know which senator it was, but it was someone suffering bad dreams and equally bad elections. Saman was able to help him with the dreams — the Megistanes practice oneiromancy, you know that? — and that seemed eventually to help with the elections, too. To cut a long story down to size, Saman received his Roman citizenship."

Arash nodded. This was not pleasant news. Upon learning his new master was a Parthian, he'd allowed himself to hope for manumission when they went to his home city. But it seemed his master was Roman in habits, or at least in those which mattered to Arash, and now they were traveling deeper into Roman territory.

"Don't carry your face around like that," said Leandros, observing Arash. "Saman's a fair man, as I said, and has a good reputation among the masters and men alike. You could do much worse than him."

"I know that's true enough." But Arash said it without enthusiasm.

"Fetch that donkey again, will you?"

Arash went after the errant beast and pushed him back into line. He glanced at the mounted soldier riding alongside the line and tried to imagine what it might be like, to sit astride a fast horse and to carry a bow and arrows which all feared. The Parthian mounted archers were justly famous.

But he was not an archer, and not a horseman. He was a slave who possessed as his only talent the playing of a woman's instrument. He set one hand against the little donkey's neck to keep him steady and kept stride with him.

Arash paused beside his master's tent wall and looked westward toward the horizon, still glowing with the last of the red sun. Above the place where the land met the sky, a scattering of stars were already shining, pale grains of sand against a darkening cloak. A few were brighter than others, but that was not unusual, stronger lights among the many weaker. Which was the star Leandros had mentioned, the one which supposedly was leading more than a dozen learned scholars into a shabby province?

"It's not visible just now," said a voice over his shoulder.

Arash jumped and whirled to face his master Saman. "Forgive me, master, I was only—"

Saman waved him to silence. "I suppose you've heard we follow a star, then."

Arash faltered. "I'd heard, yes."

"It is true. Now, come with me."

It was their first real encounter since his purchase, and Arash's stomach tightened as he ducked through the tent door, his mind racing with all the possible reasons his new master might have called him at night after leaving him unoccupied through much of the day's traveling.

But Saman hardly glanced at him as he crossed the luxurious tent. "I hope you've kept yourself well through the day. Tannaz kept you busy, I imagine."

Arash wasn't sure how to respond. "I was not over-burdened, master. I would be glad to be of more use." That seemed a good answer to please a new master.

"There should not be too much more," Saman said. "Your duties will be fairly simple. Do whatever Tannaz directs during the day, aiding anywhere your extra hands might be of use. And in the evenings, I require a musician."

This was promising. A slave playing music was not used for other night purposes.

Saman lifted a pitcher of wine and began to pour into a gilded cup. "My mind must be empty at night, and many nights my thoughts are far from clear."

Arash hurried forward. "Allow me, master," he said, reaching for the wine.

Saman waved him away. "I have other servants to pour my wine if I need it done," he said. "I acquired you for your drumming. Do you sing?"

Arash hesitated. "I — do not know, master. I suppose I could learn."

"The drumming will suffice for now. You played a soothing run at Hooshman's, something quite admirable on such an instrument. If you can drum me to sleep, I will be pleased."

This was perhaps the best Arash could have imagined. "Of course, master. I'll do my best." He drew his drum out from the new bag. "Do worries or troubling thoughts plague you at night?"

Saman opened a chest, frowned at the interior, and closed it again. "Not plague, at least not often. No, primarily I wish to sleep unencumbered and undistracted, open to the messages of dreams, and I find that music is the best way to accomplish that." He scratched at his beard. "I had a piper, who was very good, but he sickened and died before we reached Babylon. I've felt his loss keenly."

"I shall certainly do my best." Arash looked around and decided on a place against another, larger chest. He sat with his back to the chest and settled the drum in his lap; this would be a quiet song, without much movement. "Will you dream of this journey? The star, or the child, or the king?"

Saman raised an eyebrow. "You're a curious one for a slave."

Arash caught his breath. "I — I did not mean to be impertinent, master."

"No, that is not what I thought." Saman settled into his chair, propping his feet on the chest. "It is good that you ask questions, but it is unusual in a slave. Most slaves do not question, do not learn beyond what is required of them to avoid punishment." He quirked one corner of his mouth. "That is why they remain slaves."

Arash fixed his eyes on his drum and kept his hands still. Then this Saman was perhaps one who was content to let his slaves earn their freedom, and so Arash might earn his. His stomach tightened with unfamiliar hope.

"But your questions do not offend, Arash. Ask me all you like, so long as you do it discreetly and without interrupting our work."

"Of course, master." Arash's fingers flexed on the frame of the drum. "Then, if I may — why do we travel to greet a king of another people?"

"That is an excellent question, with a more complex answer than you might guess." Saman took a drink of wine. "Because long ago, this king was promised to us. Not our people, not the Parthian empire, but to our priests, the Megistanes."

Arash folded his legs before him. "How came that, master? How can a king come to the priests but not the people?"

"Have you heard of King Daryush?"

Arash shook his head.

"Let's see, he was called Darius by other nations."

Arash shook his head again.

"Well, I suppose that's to be expected. Many centuries ago, Daryush ruled with great order, setting satraps and administrators to order the kingdom. He had three men to oversee these overseers, and one of them was called Belteshazzar. He was a Hebrew, taken captive when Babylon swallowed up Israel, but our wise men have never recoiled from foreign blood so long as it serves well. Belteshazzar was made a great man and he served the kingdom faithfully.

"He also served his Hebrew god as faithfully, despite his long years in our land, and it was through this that his enemies planned his downfall. The satraps, jealous of his position and influence, devised a plan to entrap him, setting his religious loyalty against that to his king. Flattering Daryush, they led him to decree that only the king might be worshiped — an order they knew Belteshazzar would disregard. When he knelt to pray, facing his lost Jerusalem, they had him seized and brought before Daryush to be condemned." Saman stretched his arms overhead until his shoulders cracked. "They were utterly lost in their own supposed brilliance. Daryush loved and admired Belteshazzar, and he could only resent those who conspired against him and brought him to death."

The story was catching up Arash. "But the king might have saved him, had he wished."

Saman shook his head. "The king's word was absolute, above even the king. He could not alter the decree once written, not even to spare his own valuable administrator. The satraps must have believed that once Belteshazzar was gone, they would be able to sway the king to believe they had rid him of a dangerous influence."

Arash tipped his head to regard his master. "By the way you speak, that did not happen. The king did not forgive them?"

"He did not," Saman confirmed, "but wait for the story. The jealous satraps brought word of Belteshazzar's disobedience to the king, calling him by his Jewish name *Daniyyel* and citing his Jewish blood despite the fact that he had been long in Babylon and a servant of the Chaldeons. The decree demanded that Belteshazzar be flung to the lions for his supposed treachery."

"Lions?"

"The kings kept lions — a symbol, perhaps, and certainly a dramatic means of execution. You have seen the arenas for the games? Well, you know of them at least. This was less public, but just as deadly. Daryush was an old man, and Belteshazzar older still, and Daryush spent the remainder of the day consulting with the learned men and the other Megistanes, seeking a way to preserve Belteshazzar." Saman nodded confidentially. "He was one of them, after all; Daniyyel was one of the Megistanes. That is why I tell you this story."

Arash nodded, anxious that his master continue.

"But in the end, the law of the king could not be overturned, and Daryush wept as Belteshazzar was lowered into the pit of lions."

Arash blinked. "But — I thought...."

"Wait, and your curiosity shall be answered!" Saman took another drink of wine. "In the morning, at first light, Daryush rushed down to the pit of lions. He had not slept all the night, reproaching himself for his stupid vanity in following the flattery of the satraps and in condemning his friend and servant to death. But Daryush knew that Belteshazzar prayed to a long-lived god, and he hoped that Belteshazzar's god might have saved him where Daryush could not.

"And he knelt at the mouth of the pit, and he cried — we have his words preserved — and he cried, 'Daniyyel, servant of the living God, has your God, whom you constantly serve, been able to deliver you from the lions?'"

Arash was leaning forward now, intent on the story.

"And up came the sweetest of sounds! 'Oh king, may you live forever — my God has sent his angel to shut up the mouths of the lions, as I was innocent before Him.' And Daryush clasped his hands and shouted for joy, and Belteshazzar was brought up alive and unharmed."

Arash felt himself grinning. "And what of the satraps?"

"Oh, the king did not neglect them. Daryush had set out to create an orderly administration, and there was no place in it for men who would conspire jealously against those who served well — and against the friend of the king. Daryush ordered them thrown to the lions, and it is said the lions leapt and caught them before they even reached the ground, crushing and rending them as they fell."

Arash felt a delicious and faintly guilty thrill of vengeance.

"And this brings us to the relevance for our journey," Saman said. "King Daryush declared Belteshazzar's god was a living god indeed, who delivers and rescues and performs signs and wonders in heaven and on earth. And Belteshazzar continued to pray and worship even as he continued to serve Daryush and Cirrus.

"And this is the key point: this Belteshazzar was the *Rab-mag*, the chief of the Megistanes, and he dreamed and read the stars and interpreted just as we do today. He left many prophecies for the learned, including that of a messiah for his people."

The word was unfamiliar to Arash, and Saman must have seen his confusion. "Messiah, ah, *mashiach*, anointed one. A consecrated king, and in Jewish lore a redeemer."

Arash did not fully understand, but he nodded.

"Now, Belteshazzar's people are not our people, but as I have said, the wisest of us have never shrunk from working alongside the Jews, and King Daryush saw fit to declare their god is God indeed. And so for centuries, we have remembered the prophecies of Belteshazzar, our *Rab-mag*."

Arash nodded once.

"And now the time Belteshazzar spoke of has come. A great star has appeared in the west, signifying an important birth, and we have all received dreams speaking of the coming of the great king. The oracle Balaam, when called to curse the Hebrews, blessed them instead and prophesied that a star shall come out of Jacob — that is one of the Hebrew fathers — to rule all the land. That star is the king, whose star we see shining each night and follow westward.

"And how can we refuse such a call? If this is Belteshazzar's prophecy fulfilled, then we have the responsibility of it just as his own people do. We are the Megistanes, the king-makers, and we must recognize and honor this great king who has been foretold." Saman's voice became more solemn. "I do not know what manner of king this new child may prove to be. No other has been announced to us in the same way, not in all our long centuries of watching over the kingship of the Medes and Achaemenids and Parthians. We have endured through empires, and this is new to us." He met Arash's eyes. "It must be an omen of great significance. We can only guess at what we will find. But we are journeying to Herod, called the Great, to see what he may know of this. Though he deserves his title in many ways, yet he is a petty and jealous king, and certainly he will be watching closely any royal birth near his own seat of power."

Arash nodded, impressed and a little overwhelmed by the story. "If this new child is Belteshazzar's prophesied king," he asked, his voice low with solemnity, "what will you do? Will you crown him in place of King Phraates?"

Saman looked surprised. "What a bold speaker you are! But now I do caution you, young Arash, for to speak thus in the hearing of others might lead us both into danger. Certainly no slave should make so bold as to discuss the making of kings. But here in the quiet of my own rooms, I will tell you that we have not made up our minds. It is true that some of us wish to find this new king and declare him immediately, but others of us, like myself, are… It would be wrong to say that we are put off by the mighty omens of star and dreams, but we do not wish to presume this is a king-making like any other. We wish to bring gifts, to observe, and to do as we are led."

Saman tipped back his cup and finished the wine. "What a long tale you have made me tell! See where your questions will lead. And now, Arash, you may do your service by playing my mind to sleep. I must lie down quietly, with my mind open to whatever dreams may come, and in the morning I and my brothers will talk and learn if any of us have shared dreams."

"Of course, master." Arash settled the drum in his arms to mute the sound, and began to play a soft, gentle rhythm. A heartbeat of sound, syncopated yet soothing, spread through the room as Saman went to his palette bed.

CHAPTER THREE

THE days passed uneventfully, making Arash both relieved and uneasy. Each morning, he helped Leandros to pack the tents and gear and to organize their portion of the caravan. The days were spent walking westward toward Judea in slow but steady progress. Each evening, he assisted in setting up his master's tent and then, after supper, played the drum for his master.

Saman remained as personable as he had been that first night. He actually seemed pleased that his slave wanted to know more of their purpose, and he elaborated on Arash's thin knowledge of the Megistanes. They were the hereditary priests and ministers of the Parthian court, and their dual political and religious roles had been handed down for centuries, since long before the present Parthian empire. It was said the Megistanes had served four empires in succession.

They were scholars, astronomers, and astrologers, practitioners in oneiromancy and other arts. And together they elected the king of the land, naming the one who would be King of Kings on the Parthian throne. Saman, somewhere in his forties, Arash guessed, was respected among their number, but Bithisarea, Gathaspa, and Melichior were chief among those who traveled together now. Some of the others were from other orders, scholars in their own right who had also recognized the significance of the star, and the man in silks had come all the way from Serica, the land of silk.

The star had been noted by the Megistanes in Babylon, Tyspwn, and other cities, exciting them and sending them to their interpretations and books of prophecy and ultimately to gather in Babylon. It had continued to shine for a time after they determined to travel to find the subject of the star's proclamation, but a few days after they set out it had faded from view. The Megistanes were not discouraged; this was the nature of stars, and in particular of oracular stars. It would appear again if needed, and if it did not, it had done its work. The scholars could find a king, certainly, and Judea was not so fine a place that a king could easily be missed.

Saman did not press Arash to sing. Arash found he liked playing for his new master; it was easy to play for one who appreciated, and Saman enjoyed Arash's music. Arash had learned the fierce dance rhythms and energizing beats from his mother, but Saman especially valued the rapid, encompassing swell of sound which seemed to wash over the mind, leaving it clear of all but the music. This, he said, was best for both receiving dreams and taking restful sleep, and each night Arash drummed until he heard his master snoring softly, when he reduced the drumming to a whisper and then silence, leaving his master to sleep while Arash went to his own bed.

Two weeks had thus passed when one night came differently. This night, Saman had left the tent door hung wide open, and he was frowning at a large sheet when Arash entered. Arash thought it might be a map, which struck him as odd. Perhaps his master thought they had lost their way?

But though he knew little of maps and letters, the map did not look like any he had seen. "Is that where we are going?" he asked.

Saman glanced up, perplexed, and then smiled. "What, this? Oh, no. This is a map of the heavens. We cannot go there, not on our donkeys or camels or even the finest of horses." He shrugged. "Unless one considers the great ship we presently sail."

Arash sat cross-legged and rested his drum across his lap. "We'll be taking a ship? Are we going so far as the Midland Sea, then?"

"No, no, I mean our earth. We—" Saman stopped and regarded Arash with faint chagrin. "But do you not — but then of course you do not know the skies. Who would have taught you?"

Arash did not answer, because the answer was obvious.

Saman placed a date in the center of its platter. "This is the sun, let us say. And this fig is the earth." He dragged the fig in a jagged circle about the date, its sticky surface clinging to the platter. "And the earth passes about the sun, so. And thus we sail through the heavens."

Arash frowned. "But how could the earth move? It stands still beneath us."

"You're so certain? How would you know if it moved? If it has been moving all your life, why would you note it?" Saman took another fig from the tray and ate it. "Though to be honest, there is yet some argument on this point, since poor Seleucus mapped it over a century ago. But I tend to agree with him."

Arash reached out to continue the fig's sticky path about the date, trying to comprehend it. "We would feel its movement. Like an ox-cart."

"You do not feel the movement of a boat on smooth water," Saman countered.

"But I might look out from the boat and see the shore passing."

"And so we do." Saman gestured upward. "Have you not seen the movements of the stars? How they spin about us, traveling like great flocks of bright sheep? But it is not the stars which move, but we which move through them."

For a moment Arash could not speak, his mind too full of the bizarre image of the earth sailing a starry river.

"We can predict their movements, or what appears to be their movements," continued Saman, "so it stands to reason we may simply be passing through them again and again, observing them each time we pass, as they tumble over one another." He nodded toward the star map. "And when there are variations, a change in landmark — or a skymark, so to speak — we observe and listen."

"I'm sorry, master, but...." Arash was feeling keenly his low birth and simple education. It seemed incredible to even suggest that the earth might move beneath one's feet without one's notice, and yet his master took it as an unremarkable fact.

"It's all right, Arash," conceded Saman. "Not everyone knows this open secret of the world. It is hard to wonder at what has always been, and we barely think of the commonplace." He pointed at Arash. "But when we do, it can be fascinating and illuminating. For example, Seleucus posited that the tides, which vary in height and strength over all the world, are created by the movement of the moon about the earth and the earth's own spinning." He swirled his wine. "Perhaps it is something like this."

Arash shook his head and fought the urge to grin. "Oh, now you mock me, master. You are playing me for a fool, though I have done nothing to displease you, I think."

Saman smiled. "Perhaps that is a bit beyond a first lesson. Only remember this, Arash — the world is far greater than you know, and the sky holds its secrets."

Arash twisted and looked out of the open tent door. Even with their fires near, the stars were still clearly visible above the horizon. "Do they tell us everything?"

"Not everything." Saman moved and seated himself near Arash, looking out at the stars. "Often, not enough. Sometimes not even nearly enough."

Arash glanced at him, sensing something behind the words.

Saman looked at him and smiled ruefully. "And what in your simple life would you want divined, Arash?"

When will I be free? Arash thought, but he did not venture this. Not yet. Instead he said, "I'd want to know where my mother is, and if she is all right."

Saman sobered, "Ah." He looked out again to the stars. "No, I'm afraid that is one of the questions they cannot answer. And I have tried."

Arash doubted Saman had ever attempted to divine his mother's situation. Great men were not troubled by such concerns.

Saman glanced back at him, and Arash felt suddenly he had not wholly concealed his skepticism. But there was no way to beg forgiveness for what had not been said.

Saman considered and seemed to reach a decision. "I loved a woman," he said simply. "She had dark hair which curled about her ears and eyes, and she laughed like a hundred tiny bells cascading together. Her father intended her for another. When she fell pregnant, her father's chosen bridegroom turned her away, and her father was furious. He was as angry with me, I think, but he could not reach one of the Megistanes to act on his anger. But her, he could banish.

"I do not know what became of her; I never learned." One corner of his mouth drew sadly upward, a rueful half-smile. "Not a month goes by that I do not think of them, wonder who the child became, wonder where they might be. But I have found no answers, not even in stars or dreams."

Arash remained quiet. He had no answer to this, his master's private sorrows. Slaves should not see

45

weaknesses, he thought, or they might cease to fear their masters.

Saman cleared his throat. "Enough of this," he said brusquely. "I have all the long ride yet tomorrow to dwell on wrongs I can never right. Ask me a question, Arash, and distract me from memories."

Arash struggled to obey. "Er, then, if the stars cannot answer questions, why study them? They must tell something, or we wouldn't be on this journey westward at all."

"Just because they can tell only a part is no reason to disregard them wholly," Saman said. "Stars and dreams are fickle prophets. Sometimes they tell only of the great glory of creation or the innermost fears we hide even from ourselves — truths, but not answers. They are always speaking, but what they say is not always relevant."

"That is why you must look beyond the stars, to all of nature." Cao He leaned in at the tent door, smiling. "You Megistanes read only one page of a book, watching only the stars."

"Are you trying to corrupt my student?" asked Saman, and Arash looked between them and realized they were jesting. But of course they were jesting. Arash was not a student, but a slave.

"A wise teacher does not limit his pupil to only what he himself knows," Cao He said.

"Are you performing your magic tricks tonight, then?"

Cao He gestured toward his own tent. "My own poor hospitality may not compete with the sumptuous welcome of the western noblemen, but I do extend my little invitation."

Saman laughed. "Go on, then, and we will join you presently. After I warn Arash of your earth-seeking errors."

Cao He made a face of mock affront and moved on from the tent door.

Saman turned to Arash. "Cao He does not believe the earth sails the sky, as we have just discussed, but do not hold it against him. He has other qualities." He tipped his head, regarding Arash as if they really were tutor and pupil. "What do you think of him?"

Arash answered conservatively. "He dresses like no one I have seen, and he resembles no one I have seen."

Saman raised an eyebrow, as if amused by Arash's circumspection. "Cao He is a scholar like us, a practitioner of certain arts of divination and astronomy. Last year he and his fellows observed a star which appeared to hang in the sky in the west, which remained for some days and then faded away. When he performed his divinations regarding this new star, he determined it represented a great king to be born, and he chose to travel westward to discover this king.

"So he came over the Silk Road, traveling long, and at last he arrived at Tyspwn. There he stopped to confer with the Megistanes, knowing we are the most learned in the ways of astronomy and astrology, and while he was sojourning with us, another star appeared. This was not the same star Cao He had seen a year before, but it seemed to bear the same meaning, and we were able to link it with the prophecies of which I've already told you, from Belteshazzar and Balaam and others. And so Cao He came with us to seek the new king of the Jews. Though the Jews are of no consequence to him or his emperor, this king must be more than a king; his star says he is much greater. And so we will find and honor him."

Arash nodded. "He must be great indeed, if his birth draws learned men down the Silk Road." Arash had only ever heard of the legendary route and the near-mythical lands beyond, where the people wore priceless silk as everyday garments and toyed with jade baubles to amuse themselves. He had not imagined he would ever see someone from the far end.

"I think this birth is more significant than any other," Saman said seriously. "I do not pretend to understand why, but I expect to learn with time and study." He took a drink. "But of Cao He — let us take his offer to join him."

Arash rose and followed his master out into the starry night.

"Sit very quietly," Saman instructed, "and it may be that he will allow you to watch."

Arash was not sure whether his master was joking, so he nodded without answering aloud.

"I will undertake to determine if we are still traveling in a fortunate direction," Cao He said. "That is a useful thing on a journey, yes?" He raised an eyebrow at Saman, who in return gave a little sniff of mock disdain.

Cao He took wrapped bundles from a chest and laid them out in an orderly line. He carefully, almost reverently, unwound the protective cloths to reveal each in turn. First came a lacquered round board marked with lines and concentric circles and many tiny markings in an alphabet wholly strange to Arash. Next came a metal plate with similar markings, more lines than circles, and finally a large metal spoon or ladle, with a handle which looked too short to be useful.

Cao He glanced sideways and caught Arash's open gaze. Arash, startled, immediately dropped his eyes.

Cao He chuckled. "Do not be ashamed," he said in his accented tones. "I know you have not seen the like of these star maps. These are utterly unknown outside of my land, and even there only the learned in the way of wind and water use them."

Saman smiled. "The study of the stars is not limited to the Han."

"But even the wisest of your scholars do not have south-pointing spoons," Cao He said proudly. He lifted the ladle, rolled it in his hand, and dropped it over the plate. The spoon bounced and came to rest, its handle pointing toward Arash.

"That is south?" asked Saman. He held up a hand. "Don't mock me, I cannot see the stars and I'm all turned about."

"It is south," confirmed Cao He. He looked at Arash. "And now, watch this." He lifted the spoon, turned it about in his hands, and dropped it again. It fell, bounced, and skittered about again to point once more toward Arash.

Arash felt his mouth open in an appreciative grin. "Will it really point to the south each time?" He had not imagined such magic.

"Just so," said Cao He. "And now you have seen something few in these lands will ever know. Do not boast too strongly to your fellows."

Arash caught himself still grinning and glanced at his master. "That is — I'm sorry, I did not mean to stare or question."

Saman shook his head. "I would not have brought you if I wished you ignorant of such things."

But Arash did not wholly trust the assurance. Men were dishonest even to themselves, and it happened that masters promised leniency and then, when angered, forgot all such promises. A wise slave trusted only his own diligence. Arash had learned that.

Saman did not notice his reticence. "Cao He and I have been speaking a great deal about his — forgive me, even now I cannot manage the word."

Cao He smiled. "It is a *shipan*," he said, indicating the board of circles and strange characters. "We can see here how the *Taiyi*, the Pole Star, travels through the Nine Palaces. From this we can observe the five changing states of being, the houses of heaven and earth, and the sixty years of our calendar cycle."

"Sixty years!" repeated Arash, intrigued despite his inhibition. "Who should need to track so long? Surely the seasons do not last sixty years in Serica?"

Cao He laughed. "What tales they must tell of us! No, the seasons pass their own cycle in but one year, just as they do here. But we must observe the *yin* and the *yang* of each of the earthly branches, following *Suìxīng*, the Year Star. And *Suìxīng* requires twelve years to complete his august procession."

"He means Neberu," interrupted Saman. "One of the great stars. The Romans call him Jupiter."

Arash felt his master expected this to mean something to him, and so he nodded. But astronomy was the province of scholars; Arash was pleased to gaze at the stars in the night, but he did not know their names or movements.

"For all that we call them differently," Cao He said, "they are the same, and they speak equally to us. Else I would not be here tonight." He looked at Arash. "You have heard, no doubt, how I saw a broom-star standing in the west. It was visible for nearly seventy days, and in that time I searched and searched as to its meaning. I found little at first, but in the end I discovered a manuscript brought from the west, from the direction of the star, and it described a prophecy of a king who would also be a savior."

"The heavens declare the glory of God," recited Saman. "There is no speech nor language, where their voice is not heard. Their line is gone out through all the earth, and their words to the end of the world."

"Indeed," agreed Cao He. "And so I came to the Megistanes and inquired about the prophecy. And while I was studying with them, a star appeared in the sky, visible now to them as well — and *this* star was different still, a star which traveled as no other star, a star to be followed. And I am honored to be traveling with such colleagues as we seek this child." He nodded toward Saman.

"There, you see, Arash?" Saman gestured to encompass Cao He and the accouterments of his craft. "Even in far Serica, our work is practiced and our quest known. There is no doubt that this event is for all men, though the child be called the king of the Jews. I do not know how this messiah will be presented to others — but then I suppose we have waited a thousand years to see his birth, and we may wait a few more to see his purpose."

Cao He did not speak for a moment, tracing lines on the *shipan* and murmuring to himself in his own language, and then at last he nodded. "Westward," he said. "We still proceed westward." He looked up at Saman. "Likely all the way to Jerusalem, as we supposed."

CHAPTER FOUR

ARASH heard his master's voice rising above the shuffle of hooves and the snorting of horses and camels. Hugging his bag close to his torso, he jogged through the ranks of animals until he drew near Saman's grey horse.

Cao He and Gathaspa rode on either side of Saman, and it seemed the three were in fierce disagreement, though they did not express it crassly before any onlooking soldiers or servants. Arash slowed his pace and fell in behind the grey horse, not summoned after all and now slightly curious.

"It is only right that we do him the honor of a visit," Cao He said, "as it is his land through which we travel and his people whose king we ride to find. To pass him by would be an insult."

"It is precisely because it is his people's king that we should not seek him out," answered Saman. "Is it not equally an insult to say we come for another king?"

"A baby is no insult," said Gathaspa reasonably. "A baby cannot rule, and every king needs an heir. Herod has been divesting himself of heirs; perhaps news of this child would ease his familial strife."

Saman barked a sound which failed to be a laugh. "I think he may be less soothed by this news than you think. Herod hopes to establish his own dynasty."

"He certainly has a peculiar way of going about it," Gathaspa said, "executing his own sons."

"All this is beside the point." Cao He thumped his fist on his thigh. "If we go to pay homage to the future king of the Jews, we must also speak with the present king of the Jews. It is not politic? And surely this King Herod will know where to find the infant, even if it is not his own blood. That must be more efficient than wandering this—" he looked about at the dry landscape with an acerbic regard — "this empty place."

"And whatever information Herod may or may not have, he will be no hindrance to us," said Gathaspa. "He is a dog of Rome, to which he owes all. And for all that this dog may snarl in his own yard, he is toothless outside it."

Saman held up his hands. "As you say, Herod must know the location of the child, I cannot argue that. And that enough may be reason to go to him, now that the star is gone from us." He sighed. "I will agree, then."

Cao He bowed slightly in the saddle. "I will inform the others we are in agreement, then." He nudged his horse forward, his feet swinging loosely at the animal's flanks.

Arash quickened his pace to catch up to his master's horse in the empty space left alongside. Saman did not see him, as he spoke to Gathaspa. "I hope we have made a good decision. Herod is not known for his welcomes."

"Nor is he known for his independence," Gathaspa replied equitably. "He will act in accordance with Rome's wishes, and Rome does not wish unrest or abrasion between our nations. Herod will see us, and he will answer our questions."

"Hm." Saman looked forward, and he caught sight of Arash alongside. "Well, boy, you come in good time. Play us some light music to keep our pace brisk and our feet light, and we'll camp tonight within sight of Jerusalem." He reached down to stroke his horse's grey neck.

Arash fished his drum from the protective bag and began to call forth a light, syncopated rhythm which seemed to skip and leap about them. The riders and marchers straightened and looked more alert, and even the horses stepped out a bit more freely. Arash danced forward and back, playing to each row in turn, and Saman laughed and commented something to Gathaspa, who nodded in approval or agreement.

By the evening, they could see the far walls of Jerusalem, and they halted on a hill which gave them a long vantage toward the stone city. Squinting, Arash imagined he could just make out the tips of towers.

He was still thinking of Jerusalem when he went in to his master for his nightly routine. Saman noticed his distraction. "Speak, boy. You know I don't mind your questions, and I can see that you are wondering about something."

"Why did you argue with Cao He?" Arash hurried the next words, anxious to absolve himself. "I did not mean to overhear — I did not hear much. But I heard you say that you did not wish to speak to King Herod, though it is his land we pass through. And I don't understand."

Saman squinted and frowned at Arash. "Where have you been, boy? That is, what cities?"

"I had not been out of Scythopolis until I was ten, master, and then I was sold to Philadelphia. I remained there, with two different masters, until you purchased me of Hooshman."

"And you know so little of Herod the Great?"

Arash pursed his lips. "With respect, master, he is not my king."

Saman considered. "That is true, I suppose. Think on this, then: Herod was a young man when he was first appointed governor of Galilee, by convincing Mark Antony that his family's support of Brutus and Cassius had been unwilling. Entire cities were sold into slavery to fund Cassius' army, and yet Herod gilded Antony's ears with honey and gold and won his friendship." He glanced at Arash to see if the boy were following this political skullduggery. "This was after the murder of Julius Caesar?"

Arash kept still, not wanting to admit his ignorance.

"You've heard of — oh, never mind. All that matters is that this Herod is quite skilled at playing to the Romans and dancing to their pipes. A civil war between Romans became his ladder to the governorship.

"He was a brutal ruler even then; it is easy to foresee the tree if one sees the seed. Then two years after his appointment, he was displaced by Antigonus Mattathias, who won Jerusalem with the aid of Parthian soldiers and who was proclaimed king of Judea by Parthian priests. Herod's brother died, but Herod himself escaped."

Arash nodded. So his mother's people, and Saman's, had chased Herod out of Judea!

"He had to grovel to Rome, had to banish his wife and child to take a Jewish wife to curry favor with the people he was supposed to be ruling. He fought three years to take Jerusalem and to become the king of Judea."

"So he is so close with the Romans? But I have heard the Jewish people do not much like their Roman governors."

"Close? He is a genius, boy, and I say that with much dislike but with equal truth. Herod was allied with Mark Antony, remember, and shared mining rights with Cleopatra of Egypt. When Roman civil war ignited once more and Mark Antony and Cleopatra died, Herod went promptly to Octavian — you know him now as Caesar Augustus, Rome's mighty emperor — and convinced him of his loyalty, despite it having been Antony who established Herod in Jerusalem. And Octavian was not only convinced, but he even expanded Herod's rule. Yes, whatever one may think of Herod and his methods, one must admire his audacity and acumen."

Arash crossed his ankles and propped his forearms on his knees. "What are his methods?"

"A few years ago, he emptied a monastery," Saman said. "Qumran, a community of Essenes — deeply religious folk, and removed. I don't know what Herod saw in it, how he viewed them as a threat, but he has grown paranoid with age. And earlier this year, two rabbis in Jerusalem called upon their students to remove the golden eagle Herod placed in the Jewish temple, as the Jews eschew all idols and, one might think, particularly those of Rome. Herod had the rabbis and their pupils burned alive."

Arash stared. "Horrible!"

"Now, don't judge him too harshly," Saman said, and his voice took on a tone of distant mockery. "After all, the man is capable of deep love. When he left for the dangerous task of negotiating with Octavian, he feared that if he died, he would be separated from his wife, who would surely find another husband with her great beauty. So he left orders that should Octavian kill him, she should be executed at once, so that no other man might have her and Herod could be with her in death."

Arash simply stared at his master.

"She learned of this, and rather than appreciating his vast devotion, she grew to hate him. In the end, Herod tried her for treason and saw her executed, and so he grieved for a great while." Saman's voice was flippant, with a deeper undercurrent of disgust.

"I... should think he might," Arash ventured.

"He named a tower for her," Saman said. "The Miriame. It is quite beautiful."

For a moment, they both were silent. Outside, a donkey brayed.

Arash rolled his fingers across the drum skin, uncomfortable in the quiet. "I am so sorry for her."

"And her sons," Saman added. "He has killed both of them, to guard his throne. In short, Arash, this is a paranoid and vindictive man, quick to judge and quick to act, and most sensitive to all threads in the political web." He lifted his wine. "And tomorrow we ride to his palace gate, the same Parthians who exiled him in his early years and placed another king on Judea's throne, and we ask him where we may find the new king of the Jews." Saman took a drink. "And now you know why I disagreed with Cao He. It is risky to pass Herod by, and it would do no honor to him, but it is risky to approach him as well. We must hope our influence is enough to prevent his seizing us and setting us to some pretense of a trial. I doubt it would sit well with Rome if he did — they do not like him to manage such international affairs on his own — but it will be cold comfort if he is reprimanded after we are dead."

He took another drink and looked at Arash, and he was apparently amused and chagrined by what he saw in Arash's face. "Oh, come, boy, do not fret over what I say. Even Herod must remember we have a thousand horsemen waiting outside. He will not dare to interfere with us, no matter how he may stew and steam once we are gone. Now play me to sleep, so that I may dream of our journey and whom we seek."

The view of Jerusalem was clearer in the morning light, looking away from the rising sun, and Arash could make out each ornate tower.

They were still getting underway when a merchant caravan, more nimble with its comparatively few dozens of animals, moved past them on the road. Its master stopped to speak with the Megistanes. "Good morning, good sirs," said the merchant with a broad smile. "I see you are going to Jerusalem. Will you require any goods? Gifts with which to greet the king, perhaps? Or could you benefit from a guide to introduce you about the finer part of town? Jerusalem is a fine city, and there are many good families to know."

"Thank you, but we have brought our own gifts," answered Kagpha, "and we do not come to Jerusalem for business."

"For purposes of state, then?" The merchant's head tipped just slightly, and his commercial curiosity slipped over a more intense question.

"Indeed," confirmed Kagpha. "And it may be that a man of business like yourself might help us, as you must know all the relevant news and politics of the area."

"Certainly, certainly!" The merchant clapped his palms together eagerly. "You have only to ask."

Saman was shaking his head, but only Arash saw him. Kagpha did not. "We have come to seek the new king of the Jews. Do you know where he is to be found?"

The merchant's face went still. It did not quite betray fear, but its sudden lack of enthusiasm spoke enough. "The new king," he repeated. "No, I am afraid I cannot assist you, after all. Even I have not yet heard of a new king."

"He must have been born only lately," Kagpha said. "We have seen his star, and we have come to honor him and bring him the traditional gifts."

The merchant's throat worked once, and he shook his head. "I am sorry. I know nothing of this new king." He glanced forward at the road. "I am certain you do not wish to be delayed by my idle chatter," he said, "and I have customers and partners waiting for me in the city. I wish you well." He returned, mounted, and started off with his steadily-advancing caravan.

"Well done," said Saman, his voice tinged with sarcasm.

"I thought a merchant of his standing must know something," Kagpha protested. "How could it be that he would not know of a royal birth?"

A quarter-mile ahead, a camel broke away from the caravan as the merchant gestured it onward, arms moving urgently. It began pacing up the road, outdistancing the rest as its rider used the crop for more speed.

Saman nodded. "Now Herod knows exactly why we have come, no need to wonder, only plan. And all Jerusalem will be troubled with our question."

CHAPTER FIVE

THEY called him The Great, and not without reason. Certainly Herod was the greatest builder they had yet seen; he had repaired and expanded the temple, an overture to the people who did not entirely regard him as one of their own, and he built astounding fortresses. He had contributed more buildings and more beauty than anyone since Solomon the Wise.

To support his building projects, he taxed his people into distress and discontent, and his nightmen wandered ever through the city, secretly listening for talk of rebellion.

Arash had heard all these things, but he promptly forgot most of them as he trailed Saman toward Herod's palace. They were passing through the upper city, full of Roman-style houses arranged along ordered streets.

Saman laughed and nodded toward the gate of a tiled house, now nearly concealed by a number of servants bearing weapons and compressed into the doorway. "The tidings of our arrival are having their effect. It's early for flight, but the doors and windows will be barricaded."

Arash looked around and noticed other houses seeming to prepare for a mild siege. Bars were being set in windows, gate locks oiled, guards added. The arrival of the Megistanes and their search for a new king was an unwelcome flame to a city of political tinder.

The palace gate rose high and impressive from the bustling Upper Market, which should have been a wonder in itself if not for the palace wall which formed its fourth side. Guards moved about the gate and atop the wall, but there was hardly a moment of delay as they approached. Herod's men had met the Megistanes on the eastern road, welcoming them to Jerusalem and inviting them to the palace, and they were expected.

An enormous open courtyard, tiled and ringed with green plants, opened beyond the gate. On either end stood two stately buildings with columned porticoes and impressive steps. They were led toward the right. Gold shone from most of the serving vessels and decorative items about them, slaves moved in every corridor and corner, and colorful tile and stone gleamed everywhere in sun and kind shadow.

Arash took his master's sandals as they entered the palace itself, as other servants did for their masters, and then they were led to the presence of the king.

Herod was an old man, which surprised Arash. But then, he was perhaps not quite so old as he looked, as he must also be ill. He stood uneasily, hunched a little to one side as if to accommodate some deep pain, and his face was drawn in a way which even his diplomatic welcome could not conceal.

"Wise men of the east," Herod said, extending a bejeweled arm toward them. "Welcome to my court. It is an honor to receive such distinguished visitors."

Recalling Saman's explanation of Herod's previous encounters with the Parthians and Megistanes, Arash wondered if he could detect a faint undercurrent of suspicion and resentment in the king's stentorian voice. He never would have guessed at it without his master's knowledge, however, and he might only imagine it now.

"We bring you greetings, mighty king," said Melichior, "and we gratefully accept your hospitality."

For the first time, Arash realized the prestige of his master and his colleagues. They had been greeted and served respectfully of course all along their journey, catered attentively at every caravansary or given right of way at narrow passages, and he had known the Megistanes were men of rank, but he had not fully grasped what *king-makers* really meant. Their obeisances to Herod the Great were correct but easy, born of courtesy rather than supplication. These men were the successors of those who had sent Herod in flight for his life, men with a small army awaiting their word, and they were untouchable in both position and power.

But Herod was a consummate politician, as Saman had said, and even ill he did not quail before august visitors in his own hall. "My hospitality is extended as far as the eye can see, and I am pleased to count you as my guests. Tell me, what brings such scholars to Jerusalem and my palace?"

Gondophares stepped forward beside Melichior. "We have come to beg your aid on our journey."

Herod looked pleased. "But of course! I am most pleased to be able to extend my hand to the Megistanes and their companions. What can I offer you: food and provisions? Soldiers for protection? Counsel regarding some political matter?"

"It is this last," Bithisarea answered. "We seek knowledge which you must be able to provide. We have seen a star of annunciation, and we have come accordingly. Tell us, Herod, where is the newborn king of the Jews?"

There was a moment of silence, broken only by the gentle splashing of water in the fountain beyond the arches. Arash looked from Herod, his face as expressionless as one of his statues, to the Megistanes and scholars, unmoving, and he recalled Saman's foreboding misgivings. *This is a paranoid and vindictive man, quick to judge and quick to act, and tomorrow we ask him where we may find the new king of the Jews.*

"If you mean my heir," Herod said at last, his words clipped with great precision, "then it is my son Antipater who will inherit."

"I am sorry to ask you to answer again," Bithisarea said, his voice humble and steady and utterly irreproachable. "We seek a child who has come only lately. You must surely know of a king born in your own land. We have seen his star from our watches in the east, and we travel now to worship him and tender him gifts."

Herod's eyes widened slightly, but no other part of his face moved. "A new child?" he repeated. "A baby, born the new king of the Jews?"

Bithisarea's voice hesitated only an instant. "Yes, exactly so." He inhaled. "We had assumed he would be of your house."

The lower lid of Herod's left eye twitched. "I have had no son born this year. Nor any son of my sons." He drew a slow breath. "But tell me of this star, because the heavens are not mistaken in these matters."

"It was an oracular star," said Cao He, stepping forward. "My brother astronomers and I observed a *sui-hsing*, a star like a great broom, and it did not turn with the other stars, but moved alone. I knew it portended a great birth, and I followed it westward, but it vanished before I could come to the child it indicated. I went to my wise colleagues in the west, who might know more of this star and the child."

"Shortly after Cao He's arrival," contributed Gathaspa, "a new star appeared, seeming to rise out of Judea. We recalled the prophet Balaam's speech, *a star shall rise out of Jacob and a scepter out of Israel*, and when Cao He arrived seeking information about the star he had seen previously, we knew there could be no error. The events matched our own lore and prophecies, and so we have come to worship the new king."

Another quiet moment. Herod inhaled, a long, slow intake of air which Arash could hear across the eerily silent hall. "I see," he said. "I am sorry to be placed in this position of inhospitality, but I am afraid I cannot offer you the aid which you seek. This child is not mine, nor do I know of him."

Saman's fingers tightened and released, an almost-undetectable twitch. Arash felt his own pulse in his chest and ears.

"But," Herod continued, "there has been a great deal of comings and goings, with the Roman census, so not everyone is in his rightful place. And such a king must certainly have appeared in our own prophetic literature. I will call the priests and scholars of Jerusalem and put your question to them. It is quite likely they will be able to provide us an answer."

"That would be most benevolent of you," said Bithisarea. "We would be grateful for your assistance."

"I will have them called here immediately," Herod promised. "In the meanwhile, I beg you to accept my humble hospitality and entertainment. I shall have rooms prepared for you immediately."

Bithisarea bowed very low. "Thank you, great king."

They were led to a wing of cool corridors, high arches, and rippling fountains. Servants were dispatched to bring the scholars' equipment and baggage. Arash was trotting off with them when Saman's hand caught his shoulder, pulling him hard into a side chamber.

Arash swallowed against the sudden pressure in his throat, fighting the abrupt feeling of nausea. What had he done? "What is it, master?"

Saman shook his head. "I'm not angry, Arash, you've not done anything. I only want to send you — change your clothes and go into the palace. Move among the servants, aid them if you can, become one goat in the herd. But *listen*. Listen, and learn all you can of the priests' talk with the king. Some servant will hear, someone always does. Find what Herod says to them of us and our quest. Most of all, try to learn if he influences them in any way beyond the obvious, if he instructs them to mislead us. I do not wish for Herod to send us one direction while he goes more directly to reach this unexpected and undesired heir before we can find him."

Arash nodded. "I will blend with the servants and learn all I can."

"Good lad." Saman clapped his shoulder. "Off you go."

CHAPTER SIX

ARASH found a bucket and scrub brush left unattended, and he took them to carry as he moved through the palace. Thus camouflaged, he explored, trying to look purposeful and as if he were on his way to scrub a particular room. It gave him a chance to gawk inwardly at the magnificent building.

Buildings, actually; there were two main structures as he'd seen, built on an enormous stone platform to create a palace a thousand feet long. It included the *praetorium* and banquet halls, baths, audience rooms, offices, and accommodations for hundreds of guests. The arrival of the scholars had not taxed the king's hospitality or resources.

To the north stood three towers of varying heights and ornamentation. Arash wondered which was the Miriame, named for the wife Herod had loved and killed.

About the courtyard and buildings groves of trees overhung channels of water, fed by fountains of stone and bronze. Music drifted out from hidden patios and from behind fruit trees and flowering vines. Whenever another servant passed, Arash looked down and sloshed the brush and rags in his bucket, half-hiding his face, but he needn't have bothered; no one seemed to be interested. The palace was enormous, and one servant was hardly of interest to another. Security was not their concern.

It was not difficult to tell when he neared the king's quarters, however, as he began to sight guards at the mouths of corridors and at the gates in the gardens. As he approached the entrance he hesitated, wondering if the guard would challenge a menial slave on his way to scrub a floor.

"Hey, you boy," snapped a female voice behind him. He turned, sloshing water from his bucket over his feet, and a woman in servant's garb made an exasperated face. "Idiots," she addressed the portico roof. "They send me idiots, always."

"Sorry," Arash managed. "I only — the guard."

"They won't bother you so long as you do your work," she said impatiently.

Arash bit at his lip. "It's... I saw the soldiers before, you know. And I've heard...." The Romans and

Parthians had been at odds for decades, and she would probably assume Arash feared the stories.

"Persian, are you?" She pursed her lips. "Well, you had better get over your squeamishness. There are fully two thousand in the king's bodyguard, and you won't be forgiven your shirking and you can't avoid them all."

"Two thousand," he repeated. "Really?"

She nodded, a bit smug. "The Celtoi guards once belonged to Queen Cleopatra, you know. Caesar Augustus gave them to King Herod for his good service at Actium, when she and Mark Antony fell."

Arash nodded, letting his expression fall a bit blank. He probably shouldn't appear to be too familiar with these stories. "So, if I have duties near the guards...."

"You'd best do them promptly and well, without worrying about what they might be thinking. They have their work, and you have yours, and as I said there'll be no forgiveness for lazing about just because the guards are near. Now get out to that patio and scrub it clean, or there will be an answer to make. And Hiram is as likely to take it from your back as your mouth, they're that Roman here."

Arash dipped his head. "I'm sorry. I will. Thank you. I'm going." He shuffled off around the corner of the hall, glancing backward over his shoulder toward the guard, to maintain his timid fiction for the woman.

He was faintly proud of himself for feigning so well, playing the part of a nervous new servant. It hadn't been so difficult; he was nervous enough in this grand and place. But his success made him feel a little bolder. He might be a good spy for his master.

Movement in one of the garden paths caught his eye. A group of men were coming up the garden, conversing closely with both animation and anxiety. Arash had seen similar men before, in Scythopolis and Philadelphia; they were dressed in the robes and accouterments of Jewish priests.

These must be the priests and scribes the king had promised to question about the birth and prophecies. Arash had to find a way to follow them into their audience chamber and hear their discussion. That would answer his master's questions, if only he could hear.

Two young men trailed the priests, lacking the ceremonial dress and their arms full of scrolls in protective coverings. They were probably students.

Arash dashed down a parallel garden path, clutching his bucket and looking through the trees and flowers to gauge their progress. At last he cut across a corner onto a path which intercepted theirs, took a deep, panicky breath — what was he doing? This was foolish! — and hurried out straight into one of the two students.

He managed to time it perfectly, catching the youth mid-stride. The student stumbled and missed catching himself, starting to flail and then hesitating to save the scrolls, and losing in the end both books and balance. He went down, and scrolls bounced and rolled in all directions.

The second student observed in horror, jaw dropping agape, but there was nothing he could do with his own arms stacked with books. The priests whirled and their eyes widened. "Fools!" one snapped.

"I am so sorry," Arash gabbled, dropping to his knees and shoving aside the bucket and rags as he bowed. "Forgive me, my lords. Please let me help. I am such a clumsy fool, and I am so sorry."

Another of the priests reached them and cuffed Arash across the head as he started to rise. "You worthless dog! Get these collected at once! And if any of them are damaged, I will have your skin to replace them!"

For a moment Arash feared he had gone too far and risked too much, but the priest was already turning away. Arash turned on his knees and began gathering scrolls into his arms, crawling after those which had rolled down the path or against the greenery. The student was crouching with a dozen scrolls already in his arms, but instead of passing those he had collected to the youth, Arash balanced them in his own arms. "Let me help you, please, forgive me. I am so sorry."

The student gave him a foul glare, but he said nothing, and Arash rose and followed him after the priests. They passed out of the garden, up the steps of one of the palace wings, and past two armed guards who did not so much as glance at Arash as he bent his head over the scrolls he clutched to his chest.

King Herod was already in the room, pacing like a captive lion at one of the arenas. "At last, and you were a long time in coming," he growled, even more like a lion. He spoke Aramaic now, and Arash had to concentrate to pick out the snarled words. "Hurry and tell me about this newborn king of the Jews. How could I not have been informed of this?"

The priests fanned about the king and began to speak soothingly and authoritatively, their attention safely deflected from Arash. Arash delivered the scrolls to the table where the students were laying them out, and he avoided their eyes and mumbled apologies again in base humility as he slipped away. It was not entirely acting; he had come dangerously near punishment, and while he intended to be true to his master's charge, he did not mean to risk so much.

Safely out of the room, he looked about for a likely hiding place. The palace was open and airy, and the area empty but for the priests and the king. He wished for his bucket again, as it would have been useful camouflage if someone happened along to see him, but he would have to do without it.

He slipped into the next room, its doors also open to the corridor and breezes blowing in from the hills. He went to a front corner of the room and pressed himself against the shared wall. The words came faintly, but he could distinguish them.

"...Generations have passed," a priest was saying. "The prophet Daniyyel said seventy weeks of years, and—"

"Be quiet, you old goat." Herod's voice cut over the priest's. "Do not trouble or distract me with your arithmetic and generations. It does not much matter *when* he was predicted to come if he has already arrived. When this messiah-king comes, where is he to appear? That is what I want to know!"

There was a rustling of scrolls, a quiet murmur among the priests, and then one man's voice. "Let us read the words of the prophet Mikhah, oh king:

But as for you, Bet Lahem Ephrathah,
Too little to be among the clans of Judah,
From you One will go forth for Me to
be ruler in Israel.
His goings forth are from long ago,
From the days of eternity."

There was a moment's pause, and when the king spoke again, his voice was skeptical. "Bet Lahem?"

"Yes, king."

Another voice came. "That cannot be the place. Bet Laham is a sheep field, nothing more."

81

"It is the word of Mikhah," said the first priest. "Do you doubt the prophet?"

"No, but I may doubt an interpretation."

Herod's snarl cut them both off. "It's to the south, I think. How far?"

The priests faltered, clearing throats and *Hmm-ing* indecisively. It was one of the students who finally offered, "Rabbi, if I may? It is about two leagues to Bet Lahem, master."

Herod harrumphed. "It cannot be a place of consequence. It's hardly a town, is it?"

"It was a place of David, our king," said one of the priests.

Herod did not answer, and for a long minute there was nothing. Arash imagined the king stalking about the room again, the lion discontent with his own thoughts and the answers given him.

"It is near," the king said at last. "Very near."

"Very near, yes, king."

There was another moment of silent pacing. "Well, you have answered me," the king said at last. "Go. And tell no one of this supposed child or of the alleged king; I do not want further unrest in the city."

The priests departed, their students trailing with the books and scrolls, and as they passed down the corridor Arash took a slow breath. The king would go also, and then he could leave his hiding spot and carry word of what he had heard to his master.

But the king did not exit, and Arash shifted in his crouch. Was the king leaving by another way?

And then a slight, pale man approached in the corridor, visible through the door, and Arash froze. If he could see the man, the man could see him. But Arash was in the shadows, and moving would certainly draw more attention than remaining still. The man was going to the king, undoubtedly, and he would have no reason to look into the room which should be empty....

The slight man paused in the corridor, outside the doorway, and his dark eyes seemed to rest directly on Arash.

Arash did not breathe.

"Guards!" The man drew a short sword and stepped into the doorway. "Stand, and put your hands out to the side."

Arash rose, his heart pounding in his chest, and extended his arms to either side. "Please — I am a slave, I got lost — I heard the king angry, and I became frightened...."

Two armed Thracians appeared on either side of the slight man. Arash thought he might wet himself. "Please...."

The guards entered and seized his arms, stretching Arash between them until his shoulders burned. The slight man came close and dug first through Arash's bag, drawing out the drum. He examined it closely, running a hand inside the frame and testing the skin of the drum, and then dropped it to the floor. Arash bit back his protest. The man felt about the inside of the bag, searching for more, but it was empty.

Then he started through Arash's clothes, feeling for a knife or other weapon. Finding nothing, he seized the tunic and inverted it over Arash's head, sliding it over the arms as the guards expertly managed his arms through. Then he jerked the girdling loincloth from Arash's waist, stripping him, and shook it out to see if anything had been concealed within. Arash shivered with the cold air and fear.

At last the slight man looked at Arash's face. "Who are you, then?"

Arash tried to swallow through his constricted throat. "I am — I am a slave. I came with the Megistanes, I lost my way in the corridors — I am only a musician, I have hardly been in a fine house, I have only lately come to my master.... I heard shouting, I was afraid, and so I hid. It was foolish, but I have taken nothing! Please, what have I done?"

"How did you enter this building?"

The truth would serve best. "I came in with the priests. I was clumsy and I spilled some of the scrolls, and so I helped to pick them up and carry them here. But then I didn't know how to find my way out again. I didn't want to be punished. The priests will tell you what happened, if you ask them. Please, tell me, what have I done?"

"Bring him," said the slight man brusquely, and one of the guards reached for the discarded clothing as they pushed Arash forward. The slight man led the way into the audience chamber where Herod waited, scowling.

"What is this?" asked the king in his stentorian voice. "A spy? Why have you brought him to me?"

The guards pushed Arash to the floor, and he knelt with his hands in his lap, eyes on the tiles.

"Not a spy, I think," said the slight man, "or at least not a good one. He was hidden very poorly, he carries nothing of use, and he bears a drum, a noisy liability for someone intending to sneak about." He gestured, and the guard threw down the clothing.

Arash reached one shaking hand to catch his tunic and draw it across his lap. The guards did not interrupt him.

"He claims to belong to one of the Megistanes," continued the man, "He says he followed the priests in and couldn't find his way out."

"One of the Megistanes," repeated Herod. He approached, his stride less steady now that the observing priests were gone. Arash trembled and stared at the king's bare toes. "Tell me, slave, should I have you beaten for intruding into my innermost chambers, or should I have you perform a service for me?"

Arash gulped. "What service could I do you, great king?"

"Your master seeks a new king of the Jews," said Herod. He shifted his weight in discomfort, his feet moving back and forth before Arash's fixed eyes. "I will ask him to bring me word of what he finds, of course, and it is my hope that he will do just that. That would be just and proper among kings and men of state. But it may be that he will keep such news to himself, or will delay conveying this to me. And so I want you to bring me that word, as soon as you come to this child."

"How can I do that, if I am with my master in—" He caught himself. He'd nearly said *in Bet Lahem*, which would have betrayed his listening. "In service to him?"

Herod's toes faced Arash. "What is your deepest wish, slave?"

Arash's stomach twisted, but he whispered, "To be free."

"Free?" Herod's voice dripped disdain. "A worthy desire, to be sure. Do you think your master will let you earn your price?"

Arash licked his lips. "I hope so."

"Hope is a thin cord from which to hang." Herod's toes turned away. "If you bring me what I ask, slave, I will set you free that very day. That is a promise beyond what the most generous master might offer. When you have found the child, leave your master and

86

return to me in Jerusalem, telling no one, and I will give you papers of manumission and a purse to start your life as a freeman."

Arash's head jerked up and he nearly looked at the king. He caught himself, keeping his eyes at the man's torso, and clenched his fists. "I… I would…." Words failed him.

"Well?"

To be free.

To never again fear that he answered too slowly, or that he did not show himself well enough to a prospective buyer. To never again feel the sting of a strap, the throb of a cuff, the cut of a lash. There would be labor, certainly, and hard work to feed himself, but it would be his own honest labor for his own bread. And it would be *now*, in the prime of his days, not when he was thirty or forty.

And yet…. The risk was enormous, if King Herod did not keep his promise. Penalties for a captured *fugitivus* were severe, branding or flogging or other tortures. If Herod did not protect him, he could not afford to be retaken.

Though it seemed unlikely Saman would be so vindictive to the full extent of the law. Thus far his new master had done well by him, not only appreciating his music but drawing out his questions and answering them. It was possible that Saman would educate Arash if he asked it; he seemed to enjoy the discussions himself, and certainly it would improve Arash's value from being a mere drummer boy.

Yes, his master was a fine one, of which many slaves would be jealous, but even if he were willing to let Arash earn his freedom, Arash had few marketable skills and playing the drum would not pay well. It would be long years before he could expect to purchase himself.

And that limited set of skills was why he should remain with his master. He was not afraid of labor, but without a trade he would be reduced to treading urine for tanners or other menial work — and it would be better to play the drum for Saman than to stomp fresh skins for someone likely far less genial.

But Herod was a king, and he could sanction Arash's action and shield him from the law. Arash owed no particular loyalty to this new child-king, nor even to Saman, whom he had known and served only weeks. This was a priceless opportunity.

And most importantly, Arash could not refuse, not when he had been captured in Herod's palace by Herod's own guards, folded naked and trembling before Herod himself.

"I would be honored to serve you, my lord."

CHAPTER SEVEN

ARASH returned to his master late, dry-mouthed and fingers still fumbling with simple tasks like latches. He crept down the corridor and eased into Saman's room, lit by a single low light.

Saman jerked upright in his bed, his hand falling to something which flashed with reflected lamplight, and then he relaxed. "Arash," he identified. "Come in, and close that safely behind you."

Arash obeyed. "I did not mean to startle you, master."

"That's all right, Arash. I was not wholly asleep, and I have been not quite at peace here. You saw how the king regarded us."

Arash now knew exactly Herod's distrust of the Megistanes. Still, Saman's weapon surprised him and, in his present state, alarmed him. "You said Herod would not dare to open hostilities with the Parthians."

"Hostilities? No, he won't attack our thousand cavalry, certainly. But smother us in our beds? Not impossible. He had his young brother-in-law drowned at a party." Saman shook his head. "But it is most likely that I fret for nothing." He looked at Arash, tipping his head to regard him. "What happened? You look — shaken."

Arash swallowed and tried to steady himself. "No! No, I am fine. And I was able to learn what you wanted."

"Yes?"

"I was hidden within the king's audience chambers, where I was able to hear most of the king's consultation with the priests."

"Really?" Saman's eyebrows popped upward. "You show an unexpected talent for this work. Well done indeed, Arash. What did you hear?"

Arash related what had passed between the king and the priests. Saman stroked his beard thoughtfully. "Bet Lahem," he said. "Never heard of it. Doesn't sound like I would have had cause to hear of it, from what you say."

"It's supposed to be to the south."

"Well, now we will wait and see how the king chooses to inform us of the priests' findings," Saman said. "Whether he sends us to this Bet Lahem, or to some more distant village to buy himself time to address the child first." He looked again at Arash. "Once more, well done. I never expected you would get so far as to overhear the priests themselves. Herod's own night-men could not have done better."

Arash tried unsuccessfully to suppress a grin, unexpectedly pleased at the praise. "Thank you."

He pushed down the uneasy feeling of treachery. It was Saman who had sent him into danger in asking him to spy, and he deserved the lie of omission. And it was no betrayal, really, for Arash to have answered as he must when questioned by a king.

He made himself take a long, slow breath, wiped his palms on his tunic, and drew out his drum. "Would you like me to play for you now, master?"

Saman frowned. "Arash," he said, "why is your tunic inside out?"

Arash froze. When they had finally released him, he had bolted, pulling his tunic over his head as he dashed down the corridor. His loincloth was in his bag with his drum; he had not stopped running until he was across the broad courtyard.

Saman sat upright again, his eyes fixed on Arash's face. "What happened?"

"I — when I was out, when I was listening, I — that is, I was caught, by the chief of the king's night-men, I think."

Saman swore and reached for the lamp. "Arash! Are you all right? I mean, you're here, but...."

"I'm all right." Guilt pressed Arash once more as he recognized the concern in his master's face. "I pleaded that I had lost my way, being unfamiliar with the palace. He was suspicious and doubtful, but after he searched me, he finally seemed to believe me."

In the increased light, Saman frowned at the bruises already visible on Arash's wrists and forearms. "But he let you go."

Arash nodded. *Please don't ask me more.*

"I am glad. I would not have put you at such risk."

Arash turned away and brushed the drum's face quietly. "I can play for you now, since I've disturbed your rest."

Saman looked at him for a moment, making Arash's breath catch in his lungs, but then lay back. "Yes, give me some music. I wish to have all my wits for tomorrow."

They were brought splendid breakfasts in the morning. "The great king thanks you for your patience," said the servant with a broad tray of fruits and breads, "and he hopes you have enjoyed his humble hospitality."

Arash snatched a date as he carried the tray in to his master. Sucking the sweet fruit from his teeth, he thought to himself that, aside from Saman's fear of assassination and Herod's extortion of information, there was little left to be desired in the king's generous hospitality.

"A meal, yes," observed Saman as he sat down to eat, "but no word of where the newborn king is to be found. And so we wait."

They waited only until midday. Another servant came to each of the scholars, inviting them to a private audience with the king. "He does not wish to speak with you in the great hall, where all might question your purpose," the servant explained. "He has sought the priests' knowledge privately and wishes to pass it privately to you."

Saman dressed for the royal court and then gestured to Arash as he went out into the corridor to be guided to the king. Arash obediently followed, walking quietly so as not to attract the summoning servant's attention. What was not noticed would not be forbidden.

Herod was in the same private audience chamber where Arash had listened the night before. He was pacing when they drew near, but straightened and stood still as they entered, the picture of calm and stability. He did not look at Arash. Arash wondered if he had masterful control in his subterfuge, or if Herod even noticed the slaves.

"Come in, my friends," King Herod said in his deep voice. "Let me share with you what you have sought and what I have learned."

Arash kept to the rear of the room, with a few other slaves who had followed their masters. Herod did not seem to notice them, either. Arash decided Herod generally did not notice slaves.

"I have consulted with the priests and the scribes, and they assure me that the answer is quite clear," Herod continued. He gestured to a man in ornate robes. "This is the chief priest, Joazar ben Boethus."

Joazar ben Boethus gave them short greeting. "I fear you have come long for little," he said. "If only you had consulted us, we might have saved you much time and expense."

"So there is no word on where the messiah was to be born?" asked Karsudan.

"That is not entirely true," answered ben Boethus. "The prophet Mikhah did indicate that a ruler would come out of Bet Lahem. That is the city of King David, his home and where he was crowned king of Israel."

"Mikhah," echoed Hormisdas. "This prophet I do not know."

Ben Boethus looked as if he expected no less. Dryly he continued, "But today Bet Lahem is a poor town, a gathering of houses for those who work in the fields and raise sheep for Jerusalem. It is no fit place for a king to be born, especially not when Jerusalem is so near."

"Births may happen in unexpected places," observed Saman.

"Perhaps the time came upon the mother before she could reach Jerusalem," offered Cao He.

"Then certainly word would have been sent to us," ben Boethus answered. "We are not so far, and our official observation should have been required. No, the answer is Bet Lahem, but I should not waste much time on any child born in muck and sheep tracks. I am sorry you have come so far only to be disappointed."

"Thank you," said Herod, nodding to the high priest. "You have been of great help to us. You may go."

Ben Boethus made an obeisance to the king, then a lesser gesture to the Megistanes and scholars, and left the audience room.

Herod waited until the priest was gone before he spoke again. "Ben Boethus is one of those who puts great store by the things of this life," he said. "He does not trust that which is not bright with gold or heavy with coin. I, on the other hand, am more conscious of spiritual things."

"Of course," said Saman, and the skepticism in his voice was buried deep.

"I wish you to go, on my behalf as well as for your own purpose, to Bet Lahem. If this child is there, find him, and bring word to me, that I may come and do him honor and worship as well." He frowned. "I cannot leave Jerusalem just now for many reasons. I am an ill man, as you have no doubt observed, and it is most difficult for me to travel. Sitting in a chair is tortuous after a time; sitting in a jolting cart or riding astride a—" His face twisted and he cut the sentence off. "No, it's not possible for me to travel more than absolutely necessary. And think of the unrest if it were rumored that I was journeying out into the countryside to seek my heir?

"You understand, of course. I must wait and rely upon your aid, rendering help to me as I have found answers for you." Herod raised a hand. "But, when you have found the child and confirmed that yes, this is the king of whom your star speaks, then I may speak freely and publicly about the child, the foretold king of the Jews. It will settle my uneasy house and answer the weighty question of my heir, over which there has been much distress in the city and, you can imagine, in my own heart. And I will go myself to worship this new king, when I can travel swiftly and directly, and you yourselves will confer upon him all the honor he is due, making him a king in this land."

Melichior made a deep bow. "That is most admirable of you, oh king. It does answer the need for a peaceful resolution to the inheritance of your throne. We would be greatly honored to publicly confirm this king as your heir when we have found him and brought you to him."

"I am most glad to hear we are in alliance, and I anxiously await word of your search." And now Herod's eyes did shift, touching briefly upon Arash, and a chill settled unnaturally on the back of Arash's neck like iron had touched there. "I know you will not fail to inform me of what you find in Bet Lahem."

CHAPTER EIGHT

KAGPHA frowned thoughtfully. "Perhaps we misjudged the man. It is very possible, when one hears of him primarily through his deeds as told by his rivals."

Arash glanced at his master, who was listening to Kagpha, and then forward again to the road. On either side, the ground sloped away into the dry valleys which surrounded Jerusalem, as the road followed the high ridge to avoid the steep descents and climbs.

"King Herod has lost three sons to the question of inheritance already; the presentation of an heir ordained by God and peacefully confirmed by acknowledged king-makers might well appear a great opportunity for him. It would not be his own sons who inherit, but he would have one heir, not many, and he would be remembered as a great consolidator who created peace out of strife and left a peaceful transfer of power." Kagpha nodded, satisfied with this reasoning. "And he is not a foolish man."

Saman considered. "It is not what I would have supposed of him, but it is not inconceivable. Herod is an old man now, and he must be thinking of greater things than conserving his own power from a mere infant."

Arash nodded to himself, unable to disagree. He could sense his master's doubt, but also the desire to believe. It would simplify so much, including their own safety, if King Herod truly wished to honor and recognize this new child of prophecy.

Arash was walking beside his master's favorite horse, a bay gelding called Ishan. They had left Jerusalem in the afternoon, following the king's private audience and instructions; their destination was not so far that it could not be reached before dark. The majority of the cavalry was not with them; as Bet Lahem had perhaps a thousand residents, the cavalry of equal size would have overwhelmed the village and its supplies. Instead the mounted Parthian soldiers had been freshly provisioned by King Herod and would be waiting to the west of Jerusalem.

Despite Arash's logic — he had agreed only to do what Herod had asked his own master to do, and surely there could be no harm in revealing a child whom the Megistanes themselves were going to visit in open pomp — he could not shake a feeling of unease. He suspected it was a sense of betrayal, that he was stealing himself from Saman. But he was not stealing himself, he was to be freed by Herod, legally, and certainly the king would remunerate his master for Arash's small value.

Still, the unease persisted.

"What if the king's men are following us?" Arash asked finally. "You said King Herod employs secret police to guard against unrest and rebellion."

"This is so," admitted Saman with a smile, "but he would hardly need to waste them on us. Even with our reduced numbers, we are hardly difficult to track." He gestured up the ridge road.

Two hundred Parthian horsemen still rode with the Megistanes and scholars. While Herod was justly proud of his campaign against bandits on the roads of Judea, there remained some danger — and there was the greater and darker danger from Herod himself, should he yet prove untrustworthy. Thus far, however, they had seen only slack-jawed and gaping Judeans gawking at the impressive procession.

Everywhere Arash could see sheep, or signs of sheep. It was Karsudan who explained, when Gushnasaph finally commented on the ever-present sheep. Karsudan had lived in Judea for a time and knew more of their ways. "Yes, the Jews go through a lot of sheep."

"What do you mean?" Gushnasaph asked.

"They sacrifice two lambs each day in the Temple in Jerusalem, and then every household sacrifices lambs during their Pesach in the spring. Bet Lahem is good sheep country and close to the city, so the Temple flocks are kept here. This is where the sacrificial lambs are born."

Dusk was falling now over the road, and the glowing sky to the west was shaded in striking hues of blue and orange. Arash let his mind go slack, walking along the road with whatever thoughts might come free to tumble about in his head.

Freedom.

There was a sudden and widespread mutter of surprise. "Look!"

"There!"

"The star!" Gathaspa's voice rose above the general clatter of conversation and hooves. "The star! It has returned!"

Arash followed the pointing hands and saw it glowing in the southern sky — the *southern* sky! — bright against the purpling heavens and outshining the other stars beginning to glow out of the dusk. Something began to swell in his chest, something like excitement even against his better judgment. There was no point to rejoicing for a king's birth, especially a foreign king's — it could make little practical difference in Arash's life. And as ben Boethus had haughtily observed, a king born in a sheep town was hardly a king, the glorious King David excepted.

But this star, bright and brilliant, was *different*. And perhaps the king for which it shone was different as well. And despite himself, Arash's steps quickened.

The road wound southward, rising and falling over the hills, and as they wove through the turns, the star seemed to move against the sky, turning with them, leading them onward. On his horse, Bithisarea was making furious notes, cursing and laughing at his scribing errors as he wrote against the pommel of the saddle.

It was not long before they could look across the town of Bet Lahem, and the star did not yet stand still. It passed low over the horizon, glowing like a beacon, and then at last came to rest.

"I believe it is standing over a building," observed Saman, his voice quavering with incredulous glee. "What do you think, Bithisarea?"

"I agree with you," said the scholar-priest. "It is definitely over that little house — or if not standing over it, then surely indicating it. Let us go forward." He turned to call to the others. "Let us not alarm those inside, as it is certain by this town's appearance that they do not expect guests of rank. Bring the gifts, and we'll go forward alone."

He did not mean truly alone, Arash thought; even if the fifteen scholars went forward themselves without the cavalry, to avoid alarming the building's residents, they would need servants to carry the heavy gifts. The birth of a king demanded honor, with correspondingly great gifts.

Saman turned to Arash. "Fetch the coffer, if you would."

"Of course, master." Arash felt a little flicker of pleasure at his master's instruction. He might have guessed that Saman would choose him to accompany him, as he'd kept Arash close all this time, but he was newly pleased that he would see this mysterious child himself. A mere drummer and slave he might be, his only skill to play a woman's instrument, but he would accompany the Megistanes to worship this wondrous new king in a sheep town.

Arash had lived all his life in cities of the sophisticated Decapolis. They had traveled beside and through many Judean towns, but he had not thought much on them as they passed. But now, in the midst of Bet Lahem, he thought for a moment there had been a mistake — no king could be found in such a place.

He was not the only one to doubt. Basanater hesitated as they drew near. The building was a house of sorts, low in every sense from the stooped roof to its what might be generously called *rustic* construction. "This cannot be the place."

"There is a *star* hanging above it," Saman answered him, incredulous and gently teasing, "a star which has traveled before our eyes. You may have so little faith in prophecy, but do you also doubt your own astronomy?"

Basanater smiled with embarrassment. "I suppose we have followed it this far," he admitted. "It would be foolish to disbelieve now."

Their steward Tannaz knocked at the door and called for entry. The man who opened froze and gawked for a moment, nearly pushing the door closed again in his surprise. Tannaz prevented this insult by planting his foot solidly in the way.

"What could I do for such lords?" jabbered the man, blinking around at them. He glanced toward the edge of town and then back, leaping to a conclusion. "I know the caravansary is full to bursting, but this town is not for the likes of you. I do my best by all strangers in the land, I observe the holy law of hospitality — but I could not accommodate such fine guests, even had I the room. I have only a country home, forgive me."

"We do not seek shelter for the night," said Melichior. "We come in fact for a child. We are looking for an infant, not too old, who is born the new king of the Jews."

The man did not seem to understand. "There are no kings here," he managed.

Melichior was more patient with him than many might have been. "You might know him only as a child," he said. "Do you have such an infant in the house?"

"We do," said the man. "The carpenter's boy." He looked around at all of them again.

Melichior's patience began to show the barest of wear. "Go and tell the carpenter and his wife, then, that we wish to see the child. We have come to worship him and bring him appropriate gifts."

This pronouncement seemed to be beyond the man's comprehension. "To see the boy?" he repeated. "Here?"

"If they will allow us. Go and ask them."

The man gaped unmoving, his mouth working once, and Saman stepped forward. "Lead us to them," he said firmly, stepping into the door.

The man hurried backward to keep clear of the rich clothing, and Saman followed him into the room. The man bowed low and then hurried back to a rear room. "Yosef!" he called. "Yosef!"

A short, dark-haired man opened a door as they drew near. He started to speak to the owner of the house, but stopped wide-eyed when he saw Saman and the others coming along with him.

"Are you the carpenter?" asked Gathaspa. "Have you a newborn son?"

Yosef nodded. "I do."

"We are the Megistanes, and we have come to pay homage to him and to worship him."

The infant lay in a bundle of blankets on a low mat in the corner of the room. A slight, dark young woman seated nearby was curiously watching the doorway and as they entered, she looked startled and pushed herself to her feet.

The room was narrow, and the servants could not follow their masters into it. Melichior, Gathaspa, Bithisarea, Cao He, Saman, and the others arrayed themselves before the sleeping child and prostrated themselves to the floor. The dark young woman, just visible to Arash through the slanting door, caught her breath and clapped a hand to her mouth. Yosef looked solemn and awed.

The priests and scholars rose, and Bithisarea turned to gesture a servant forward. "We bring gifts for the new king," he said. "We hope these will be both of use and of honor."

They had all brought items common among gifts to royalty and deity: Bithisarea, Gondophares, Hormisdas, Basanater, and Badadilma had each brought myrrh, and Cao He, Gathaspa, Larvandad, Hor, Kagpha, and Badadilma had brought containers of frankincense. Both of these were aromatic resins which were greatly prized. Perfume, incense, anointing oil, spice, and medicine all at once, these were kingly gifts. The others, Melichior, Gushnasaph, Karsudan, Badadakharida, and Saman, had brought gold, the ancient gift of wealth.

Arash came forward with Saman's weighty coffer of gold, kneeling with difficulty to place it alongside the multi-colored globular pellets of myrrh. This gift was also traditional, and as clearly valuable. It was, Arash thought privately, also more immediately practical for a child sleeping on a mat in a corner of a tumbledown house.

Surely no king had ever been found and honored in such low conditions?

The baby was no longer a newborn. Arash was not experienced with children, but he guessed the child to be about two months old. He slept with his mouth open, a bit of drool glistening on his cheek. He did not look like a mighty king.

Melichior was speaking to Yosef. "And so you came to Bet Lahem?"

"But there were so many here, there was no room — even our own family could not provide for us here. Though it was hard to ask it of them, as she would make them all unclean with the birth. And when she came into time.... It was frightening, I am not ashamed to admit it. Shemu'el found us a midwife, and as all the rooms were occupied and as she could not defile the house, we went to the tower with the sheep, where the Temple lambs are birthed. We had to put him in the manger, for a place to lay him. That was just as well, it gave her some privacy in the end. But I was glad when other travelers began to start for their homes, and we were able to move in here."

Arash couldn't stop himself from staring first at Yosef and then at the sleeping baby. Laid in a manger? It was unthinkable. Even the slaves' children were not born alongside the sheep and goats. Surely... surely a king who was born in such conditions must be different. Surely a king who came out of such a birth would think of all people.

Suddenly, Arash wished he had a gift to proffer like his masters. If this king were not merely a king of the Jews, but as Saman and the others said, a redeemer of the oppressed and lost, then Arash wanted him to be *his* king, too. And he wanted to make a gift to the strange pauper-king.

A slave had few gifts to offer, however, and Arash remained still.

The dark young woman started forward past the rich offerings, her arms reaching toward the baby as if to bring him to the visitors. Melichior held up a hand to forestall her. "Please, do not disturb the young king," he said. "We are come to pay him honor, not to disrupt his sleep."

She smiled at that, shyly.

Yosef was looking up and down the array of gifts. "We were in Jerusalem only a week ago," he said. "For the redemption of the firstborn." He shook his head in wonder, staring down at the coffers and jars. "If we had even just a bit of this at the time of presenting him, we would not have been limited to the two turtledoves for a poor man's son. We could have dedicated our son properly."

"He was dedicated properly," said the young woman. Her tone was gentle — not a rebuke, but effectively correcting her husband's statement. "He was redeemed according to the law, and he was blessed by that righteous man Shimon and the prophetess."

"Of course," Yosef agreed, and his smile was both abashed and appreciative.

The infant stirred and made a few choking cries, his voice catching in his throat. Now the young woman did go to him, catching him up gently and cradling him in her arms. It did not forestall the cry, and she turned to bare her breast for him. But the baby did not take the teat either, and his thin wails rose to full shrieks.

The young mother's face screwed up in distress. "Take it," she whispered. "Don't cry, little one."

But the infant continued to cry, moving within his wrappings. Yosef moved to join his wife. "Is he ill?"

Gathaspa scooped up a handful of frankincense tears, rolling the multi-colored nuggets in his hands. Bithisarea opened a jar of myrrh and poured it from one hand to another. "Look, little king! Look at these!" they crooned. "See how they are all different? Don't they smell delightful?"

The child cried, his face reddening.

Melichior cupped his hands into one of the coffers of gold. "Look, child! See the faces? This is Phraates, the Parthian king of kings, but you will be the king of all kings. See how it glisters? Smile, little king!"

The child wailed more loudly.

The parents leaned close over the crying child, and the wise men watched helplessly, their hands starting and hesitating as their learning and power availed them nothing.

Arash reached into the ever-present bag slung over his shoulder, his fingers closing about the familiar curve of his drum's frame. This... this he could give. He had no right to assert his music here — but he had nothing else to offer this king of all people, no fine gift like his master's and the others. Nothing but this.

He swallowed and drew out the drum. No one saw. The baby shrieked. With his heart in his throat, Arash began to play.

A few finger-strokes brought a soft tremor of sound, and all eyes turned sharply toward Arash. Tannaz shot an angry glare at him, but Arash did not meet his eyes. He did not look to see his master's expression. He looked at no one but the child.

He strengthened the beat and increased the volume, and the crying infant hesitated. Arash made the little drum give a short, muted boom, and the baby stopped, his mouth open, his head turning to seek the sound.

Arash dropped the volume and played a rapid syncopated patter, slowly growing in intensity, and the baby listened in open-mouthed wonder. Arash made the rhythm dance and leap, tones high and low. The young woman moved her head in time with the lively music, smiling a little. Yosef tapped his fingers on his wife's shoulder.

Arash began to move, weaving a little with the percussion, varying the timbre, striking the drum with finger and palm. The Megistanes and scholars spread a little, actually clearing a space for him as he skipped a little in place. He took a few steps forward, dipping with the thrumming song, feeling his cheeks swell a little as the joy of the music rose in him.

He looked at the baby, the tiny King of Kings, a messiah sent by a God who closed the mouths of lions and marked the birth of the promised redeemer with a traveling star. He smiled at the infant king who was born in an animal stall and reared in a tattered guest room to rule the world. And he played.

He played with all that was in him, pouring his longing for freedom and his hope for opportunity into the music, his love of his mother and his wish for a father and his wild, dangerous, slippery desire to believe there was a God who would send a holy infant into the lowest part of the world for the redemption of all people.

The infant's eyes were unfocused, not tracking the drummer boy dancing about the crowded room, but he lay silent and awed at the music, blinking upward. Arash slowed the beat, letting the timbre fall, bringing the rhythm to a slow heartbeat, a soothing trickle of sound that drifted and settled slowly into quiet. The baby smiled, his tiny face crinkling with pleasure, and he fell asleep against his mother's torso.

CHAPTER NINE

"THAT was impressively done."

Arash, leaning against the pale slanting stone of the house, looked up and started to his feet as his master spoke. "I'm sorry, I didn't—"

Saman held up a hand. "Be at ease."

Arash stood anyway, uncomfortable in the presence of the master he was to betray.

Not betray. Leave.

"I am going back to our camp," Saman said. They had set up their tents and picket lines outside of the town, and all evening townspeople had been observed coming to peer at the travelers and their animals. "Do not hurry back for me; I expect my mind will be at peace this night even without your music." He looked at the sky, speckled brightly with stars, but now lacking the most brilliant.

Arash's heart quickened at the release of his duties. "Then I may remain here for a while?" he heard himself say.

"Of course. Come back when you're ready to sleep." Saman turned and started away toward the lights of the camp.

Arash rubbed his hands over his arms, wishing he had thought to retrieve another layer of clothing before his master went to his tent. Now he would have to depend on his movement to keep warm through the night.

His drum was still in his bag, slung over his shoulder and chest. The sky was bright with stars to guide him northward, and there was enough moon to keep him from tumbling off the road. While most slaves went barefoot, Saman had permitted Arash sandals for their traveling, which would lend him speed in the dark. King Herod had greatly reduced the number of bandits on the roads, and anyway they would generally be watching for prey during the day, when travelers were more likely to be about; by night, even the bandits would be settling in their encampments and villages. There was nothing to stop him.

He was only going to tell the king where to find the child. Herod had every reason to know, and he said he wished to honor the newborn just as Saman and the others had done. Arash was only going to do what Herod had requested of his own master. That might even be considered a service to Saman, answering the king's request more quickly. A final service before Arash took his freedom.

Arash smoothed the strap of his satchel and stepped away from the wall, walking northward to Jerusalem and to Herod.

He had just sighted the grey walls of Jerusalem when the latchet of his sandal snapped, sending Arash into a tripping series of steps. He caught himself before striking the ground and, broken shoe in hand, moved to the side of the road to sit upon a suitably-sized rock. By the light of the moon, he examined the broken strap and knotted it into temporary repair. The result made a slight lump beneath the ball of his foot, but it held as he walked.

The carpenter said they had been in Jerusalem only a week before, to sacrifice for the firstborn. Clearly they did not fear Herod. He did nothing wrong in speaking of them to the king.

Arash had made good time covering the twisting, hilly road from Bet Lahem to Jerusalem, but it would be very late when he arrived. Surely the king would not see him until morning. But sleeping on the open road seemed less secure than walking upon it, and it was cold beside. And sleeping in the lower city's streets would be foolish, begging for robbery, so he would go to the palace despite the hour. They must be used to messengers arriving at all hours.

The city gates were closed, but a yawning guard answered Arash's call. "I come with news for the king," Arash explained. "I must get to the palace."

"You?" The guard looked dubious.

"I would not dare to lie about such a thing."

The guard was unimpressed, but he turned and called to another. The little door in the gate was opened to admit him, and the night guard pointed to an armed and armored soldier. "He will escort you to the palace, so you had better be speaking the truth."

"I am," Arash assured him, but again the guard did not seem to care. His duty discharged, he locked the little door again and dismissed Arash from his mind.

Arash and the soldier wove through the streets of the lower city, unnaturally still in the night with occasional sounds muted by darkness and closed doors. Arash was grateful for the soldier, as he doubted he could have found his way through the labyrinthine alleys by himself. They passed through several market spaces, empty where there should have been leather, cloth, dried fish, pottery, bread, perfumes, and animals for sacrifice, all available for sale. Arash had never realized how eerie the emptiness of night could be.

At last they passed through another gate and emerged into the upper city, where the cramped and twisting maze gave way to broad and orderly Roman streets, neatly arrayed in grids and straight lines. Great houses lined the streets, the homes and businesses of the powerful. They passed the semi-circular theater, ghostly in the moonlight, and went on to the magnificent upper market, surrounded by a two-story portico and as surreal and empty as the bazaars in the lower city.

And then they were at Herod's palace itself, and the guard beat on the door with the hilt of his *pugio*. "A messenger," he called gruffly.

Arash hoped they would admit him, that the slight, pale man would acknowledge his errand. If not, what would be done with a slave boy who claimed royal business in the middle of the night?

But the guard who answered the door was neither surprised nor suspicious. He admitted Arash and pointed him toward a corner without speaking. Arash went to it.

A moment later a man entered the tower room. Arash had not seen him before. "You come with a message?"

"With information," Arash modified. He spoke as he had been instructed. "I come at Aegaeon's request."

"Ah." The password seemed to satisfy the man. "And is it urgent, or will you deliver it in the morning?"

Herod had said to return immediately, but he would not be pleased to be woken. The news was not urgent; the baby would be in the inn yet in the morning. "It can wait."

The man nodded. "Then come this way, and I'll give you a room for the night."

The room was small, and the bed was narrow, but it was for Arash alone, and so was luxurious. A pitcher of watered wine and a loaf of bread were set to one side with a bit of dried fish. Arash sat cross-legged on the bed and grinned around at the room. When he had his freedom, he would have such a room every night, all to himself.

He ate and drank first. Then he massaged his foot, bruised with the knotted latchet, and settled his drum safely in the corner behind his head, furthest from the door. Then he lay down, and sleep came quickly.

He dreamed first of drumming, which was not uncommon for him. He dreamed of riderless horses, running across the desert, manes and tails streaming behind them. He dreamed of crowds pressing around him, jostling his drum, stepping on his feet, carrying him through a market where he did not want to go, where around him perfumes and dried fish and garments and slaves all were bartered and sold.

And then his dreams changed, shifted to something more imminent than even his most vivid dreams.

At first he could see nothing through a heavy darkness, but he heard the crying of infants — not just the child he had seen in Bet Lahem, but many infants, all wailing together in terror and pain. Over them and even louder was the sharper wailing of women, first the panicked shrill screams of fear and then the ululating wails of sorrow and mourning. Sight joined sound, and he could see the women keening as they rocked and clutched bloodied bundles to their breasts.

One woman, dressed in peasant garb, dashed through the darkness, bent over a baby which screamed with his mother's fear and grabbed at her robe with small fingers. A man rose out of the dark in pursuit, catching the woman by her hair and flinging her hard to the ground. She shouted in protest and kicked at him, shielding the child with her arms, but he caught it one-handed and lifted it shrieking into the air. With his other hand he swung a sword, cutting deep into the little body until the blade stuck. He released the child and shook it loose from the sword, letting it fall onto its mother, who stared wide-eyed and screamed.

Arash spun, finding himself in the midst of carnage. All around him women ran carrying their children, or wrapped themselves around their babies to shield them, or fell on their knees to beg mercy of the relentless men with swords. All failed, and the men slew child after child as their mothers wept. A peasant man ran in front of a woman and child, a scythe in his hand, but the night-men with swords cut him down, wresting the child from the wide-eyed woman as she watched him fall.

Arash wanted to run — wanted to push a mother ahead of him into the blanketing darkness, wanted to seize a child and bear it safely away, wanted to flee the horrific scene and leave it far, far behind him — but he could not move. He could only look about him and watch children die.

And then he came awake, jerking upright in the bed and choking on screams he could not utter, his pulse pounding in his ears and the scent of blood so thick upon him he could taste it. His hands shook as he grasped for his satchel and he clutched his drum to his chest like a charm, as if it could ward off the dream.

For a long moment he sat in the dark, panting, clenching his fingers about his precious drum, trying to sort the darkness of the dream from the darkness of his room. It *had* been a dream; he was alone in the small room, and there were no children, no mourning mothers, no night-men coming to murder the innocent. His sweat cooled on his face and arms, making him shiver.

Saman would understand it. Saman and the other Megistanes were oneiromancers, practiced in dreams and their interpretations. But no, Arash told himself. There was only one infant, and he was safe in Bet Lahem. Arash had not seen the newborn king or his parents in the dream, so the dream could not be about him. Arash clung to this thread of logic, though it did not comfort him.

The Megistanes said it was possible to tell the future from certain dreams.

Someone tapped at his door, and Arash jumped in his bed. "Yes?" he called, his voice scratching and hoarse as if he'd been screaming.

The door opened, admitting lamplight which made Arash squint and duck, and the man who had met him at the gate entered. "Do you come with word of the Megistanes and their errand?"

Arash nodded. "That's right."

"Fool! Why didn't you say so? The king has been up all this night with worry for news of them. You should have gone immediately to him. On your feet, and come with me now!"

Arash nodded and forced his fingers to uncurl from the drum. "I'm coming."

CHAPTER TEN

ARASH stood against the wall, wiping his damp palms occasionally against his tunic. The weight of the drum hung solid in the bag on his shoulder, and irrationally he wanted to take it out and hold it again, to press the comforting skin and wood in his hands.

Herod entered the room again like a lion, even to his snarl. "They should have returned by now," he rumbled to the slight, pale man on his left. "Are they keeping me from him? Do they mean to enthrone him even as a child, to set him against me so quickly?"

"Perhaps they are yet returning," suggested a second man on the other side of the king. "They might have stayed the night near Bet Lahem. Or perhaps they could not find him immediately; they did not leave Jerusalem early and they would have arrived at Bet Lahem near the evening. They might spend another day in searching."

"It cannot be so difficult to search Bet Lahem," snapped Herod. "It has barely a thousand inhabitants, I am told, and none of them candidates for kingship." He hunched slightly, one forearm against his lower abdomen, and his face twisted as he walked. Herod's pain brought out the viciousness already in him, Arash realized. A savage creature indeed. "And it is only a few hours' travel, even if their beasts are burdened by sumptuous gifts for the new brat."

The slight, pale man, chief of the night-men, gestured toward Arash. "We have no further need to wonder, king. The slave is returned."

Arash's stomach clenched as Herod turned on him, and for a moment his throat seemed to stick closed.

"Well?" demanded the king. "Speak! Where did you find the child? Who is he?"

Arash licked his lips, but it did not aid his voice.

"Speak, or I'll have you flogged! If you will not use your tongue, I'll have it torn from your head! Where is this supposed king?"

Arash saw the tiny, helpless infant, wrapped in cheap cloths and lying on a mat in a tumbledown house, watched over by a carpenter and a woman no older than Arash himself. He could not betray them to this jealous, paranoid madman. "I — I don't know."

Herod's eyes burned into Arash. "How can you not know? Did you not accompany your master to seek this child?"

Arash dropped to his knees. "I do not mean to contradict you, mighty king. I did travel south with my master to Bet Lahem. But I did not go into the town to find the child. I do not know where he is."

Herod closed the distance and struck him hard across the face. "You were to find him and report to me! What use are you? I should have your skin whipped from your—"

Arash flung himself to the floor, palms flat, his forehead and nose pressed hard to the cold stone. "I am worthless, I have failed you," he pleaded. Groveling often succeeded where no measured protest would — though he was beginning to understand now that he would not have survived to bear witness of Herod's treachery even if he had performed the service perfectly. He had been a gullible fool. "But I could not fulfill your order. Why would they take me to greet a new king of kings? What slave may approach a king? What king would suffer a slave to offer a gift?"

The infant smiled.

Herod kicked him once in the shoulder. "No slave may approach a king," he said resentfully, disgusted at the plausibility of Arash's protest.

"But we know they went indeed to Bet Lahem, and found him there," said the slight man. "He has confirmed that much."

"Then send the night-men to Bet Lahem. Find him and kill him."

Arash, face still to the floor, stopped breathing.

"They must expect that you might know of him," said the other man. "They might place the child among the young of Bet Lahem, hoping to hide him among the peasants."

"There can't be so many male infants," said the slight man. "Certainly no more than two dozen, in a town of that size."

"Then kill them all," returned Herod. "That man from Serica said he first saw a standing star over a year ago, didn't he? That might have been the first sign. Two years then — every male child under two years of age, in Bet Lahem and around the town. Send your night-men and have it done."

Babies crying, women shrieking, a man falling in blood—

Arash pushed himself from the floor, running for the door even before he was upright. Herod shouted, the slight man sprang after him, but Arash bolted through the door and ran.

The room opened onto a colonnaded corridor. Arash slapped the far wall and stumbled forward. The slight man hit the wall immediately after him, a leaf-bladed *pugio* clinking into the painted wall where Arash had been. Arash ran.

His arms pumped as he skidded through the porches, dodging about the great columns. Shouts echoed through the halls and feet pounded behind him, but Arash did not look back. It would only slow him, and knowing exactly how many armed guards pursued him could not make him any faster.

The walls about the palace were high and even if he could somehow scale them, he could never manage before the guards caught up with him or alerted the others. And as expansive and many-roomed as the palace was, he could not hope to hide within it. His best hope was to escape out the gate by which he had entered.

He slipped and darted to the side as he burst upon the open courtyard. Running directly across would be fastest, but he would be most visible from behind, and the guards at the gate would see him pursued and would seize him. He ran instead for the roofed walkways and then down to the garden which lay between the open patio and the wall. He ducked low and ran bent, clutching his drum satchel to him, half-crouched behind the flowering bushes. The fountains helped conceal the sound of his passing.

But there were only so many places he could flee, and guards were streaming out of the high building behind him now. They paused in the portico to scan the courtyard and then spread across the patio, moving toward all the gardens and the far building.

Arash abandoned caution and bolted for the gate. "Open the door!" he called. "An urgent errand — Aegaeon's request! Open the door! I can't be delayed!"

A guard leaned out of the tower arch and looked toward Arash, who gestured frantically. "The door! Hurry! Aegaeon's orders!"

Whether he recalled Arash from before, or whether it was the phrase which suggested night-men business, the guard turned back into the tower and Arash heard the heavy clink of a bolt sliding. A fresh burst of speed brought him into the tower and he panted, "Lock it!" as he dashed past the startled guards and into the Upper Market.

But already guards were shouting from the palace behind them, and the tower guards did not close the door. "Wait! What errand?"

Arash did not slow, did not veer. He ran directly across the market floor — of course they had seen him now — and through the opposite side.

The broad lanes of the upper city stretched before him. He went left first — north, he realized too late, toward the citadel he'd seen when the Megistanes had come into the city. Full of soldiers, and not where he wanted to find himself trapped against Jerusalem's wall. He took the next right, shielded now a bit from the pursuing soldiers' eyes.

The grey-yellow stone gave back enough moonlight that he could run at speed. He ran past the houses of the wealthy and powerful, eying their high walls and locked gates with despair. He needed a place to hide; he could hear the guards' feet and voices behind him.

The amphitheater rose out of the dark, and Arash ran along its curved facade hoping for an entrance. His bare feet were stinging with impact and scrapes. No gate had been left unlatched, however, and his breath sobbed in his throat.

The gate to the lower city was open.

Without waiting to learn why, Arash bolted for the little door in the gate. He sped into the lower city and straight off the main street and into the warren of precariously stacked buildings.

Shouts of anger came from the guards behind him; they knew how difficult the lower city could be. Arash could become a mustard seed in a field if he slipped deep enough into the lower city.

But Arash was a stranger to the city, and he could not simply disappear into it. He ran along the increasingly narrow paths, twisting and turning, hopelessly losing his sense of direction, until he was in an alley of a single arm's width. He spun to search for escape, afraid the alley would end in a joining of walls and leave him trapped, and then he seized upon stones in a jutting corner and began to climb.

The roof tiles were in only fair repair, but they held beneath Arash's weight as he started along the rooftop. He bent low as he moved. The narrow streets would prevent the guards' seeing him until they were very close, but a lucky glance might catch him silhouetted against the moonlit sky.

From his high vantage point, he could see the roofs slope down toward the south. That was the direction he should go to get back to the Megistanes and his master — if he could return. He had fled his master. He was now a *fugitivus*, and Saman would be well within his rights to turn Arash over for judgment.

But Bet Lahem was also to the south, and Arash had to warn them all. Herod's night-men would be coming to kill the children, and Arash was the only one who could warn their mothers to hide them.

"He was here," came a voice clearly.

Arash flattened to the roof, holding his breath.

"I saw him come down this way, but I lost sight of him as I ducked under the laundry line. He has to be hidden near here."

"Do you think he went in somewhere?" Another guard pushed experimentally at a door. It did not open.

Arash dug his fingers into the tiles. He could not move without their hearing the scrape of the terra cotta. He needed to distract them, to send them another way before they thought to search upward.

"Look here," one said. "Think you could climb this? I'll bet he did."

Arash's chest spasmed, and he looked desperately around for something, anything. He could not pry loose a tile without betraying noise. He seized the satchel with his drum. *No!* But there was nothing else.

He pulled the bag over his head and squeezed his eyes tightly shut for a moment. His breath caught in a way that had nothing to do with his flight. Then he flung the bag back-handed over the row of roofs. It struck a far wall with a reverberating thrum and bounced to the alley below.

"What was that?" The guards started down the alley, seeking a link to the next path, and Arash began crawling along the center of the roof. He heard their triumphant cry upon finding the satchel — "he must have heard us and bolted from his hiding hole" — and their quick discussion. One began beating on a door, plainly suspecting Arash of hiding in a local shop or house.

Arash crawled southward from rooftop to rooftop, the leaning houses and sagging lines making it easy to pass from one building to the next. The sounds of the guards were muffled by the crowding buildings and the disgruntled or frightened sounds of the houses waking at their knocking. Arash left them behind and worked his slow way south.

When he came to one of the main thoroughfares of the lower city, a proper street through the tumble of housing and shops, he had to descend. He pressed himself to a shadowed wall and looked both ways, listening hard, and then ran for the shadows of the far side of the street.

His sandals had been left in the little room — shoes were not worn indoors, and certainly not by slaves before kings — and one foot was badly abraded from climbing the stone. He kicked some dust into the scrape to stop its bleeding and then started southward again, staying within sight of the main street but weaving through the side passages as much as possible. His shoulder felt strange without the familiar weight of the drum, and he pushed away the thought before it could sting him to tears.

At last he could see the outer wall, and he slowed to breathe. Nearly there! If he could think of a way to get through the gate, something to convince the guards to let him out in the middle of the night.... He wondered if the phrase which had admitted him to Herod's palace might also be recognized here.

He edged along the street until he was within eyesight of the south gate. He swallowed and rubbed his hands on his tunic, leaving muddied streaks. What could he tell the gate guards? He would just have to try the name Aegaeon once more, and hope that no word had yet reached this gate to forbid all spies' exits.

He straightened, took a steadying breath, and stepped forward.

A clatter of hooves interrupted him and he darted backward into the shadows. A half dozen horses came down the street bearing armed men.

"Gate!" shouted the foremost man. "King's business!"

Arash knew the grim-faced men. He recognized them from his dream. These were night-men, sent secretly to kill the male children of Bet Lahem.

The gate was opened just enough to admit the horses, and the men rode through in single file. Arash took a step forward as if to stop them — but they were six armed men, and the gate guards beside. And then they were through, and he could not have caught their horses. His legs went watery beneath him and he sank down to the dusty stone street.

The gate closed, cutting off the sounds of the horses' hooves on the road. Arash was trapped within the city, but it no longer mattered.

CHAPTER ELEVEN

THE city began to stir around him as the sky lightened. The bakers rose first, starting the day's wares early in the ovens. Then other vendors began to set up their shops to open, and still Arash sat in the street, slumped against a wall near the main thoroughfare.

He had run away from his master, a good master, to aid a jealous and murderous king. He had fled the king, making himself a fugitive twice over, and yet failed to warn Bet Lahem. And the little carpenter's son who was somehow a king of more than the Jews by now had died at the hands of Herod's night-men. Arash had no freedom, no master, no drum, and no king.

At last the gate in the wall opened to traffic, and Arash pushed himself wearily upright. His torn feet had swollen as he rested, but he should leave Jerusalem. It was likely the king's men were still looking for him. He could not bear to go all the way to Bet Lahem, not now, but this was the nearest gate, and the road must lead somewhere.

He was not questioned by the guards or publicans, who assumed him on some errand for some merchant master; he plainly carried no goods to tax. Arash shielded his eyes from the sun streaming over the eastern hills and started down the road, stumbling a little as the stones bit at his feet.

Traffic passed him in both directions, but no one spoke to him. He was glad. He did not know how he would speak to anyone, now that he had the blood of so many infants on his hands. Herod might have ordered their deaths, but couldn't Arash have warned them? Couldn't he have lied to the king about the location of the child?

And Arash was a *fugitivus*, a runaway slave. Anyone might seize him, once Saman had put out word that he had stolen himself. No, Arash could speak to no one.

By the time the sun had reached its zenith, Arash's throat was burning with thirst and his feet were bleeding. Wearing sandals on the journey had softened them, and he resented Saman for ever having let him have shoes. He wished for water — he'd had nothing since the watered wine the night before, and his night flight had left him thirsty even before he began walking — but there were no streams along the high ridge road. He held an arm over his eyes to block the sun as best he could and stumbled on.

His name was repeated several times before he recognized it. "Arash! Arash! Can't you hear me?"

He gave a little start and looked up at the horse and rider cantering toward him from the south. It was Ishan, bearing Saman. Arash tried to turn and run, but he tripped and went down among the rocks.

"Arash!" Saman swung down from the horse and let the reins dangle. "By all that's holy, you look terrible. Drink something before you speak."

He put a leather bag into Arash's hands, and Arash stared stupidly at it. Then he raised it to his mouth and gulped greedily.

"Steady," warned Saman. "You don't want it all coming up again. Terrible waste."

Arash lowered the bag and wiped his mouth. "I'm so sorry," he said, or tried to say. His voice shook.

"The young king is safe," Saman said. "Know that first."

Arash stared up at him, not daring to believe. "How?"

"We all dreamed," said Saman, "all of us together, the same dream. We were warned not to return to King Herod as he had asked. And the carpenter had a dream, in which an angel also warned him of danger from King Herod. He immediately took his wife and child and set out to the west." Saman glanced in that direction, as if he might see them. "I believe they will take refuge in Egypt. At least now they have the funds to travel safely and to stay for a time out of Judea."

Relief poured through Arash like the water. But it was not enough.

He nodded. "I had a dream, too." He licked his cracked lips. "But I was too late, or at least I could do nothing about it. I tried."

Saman was solemn. "The horror in Bet Lahem?"

Arash nodded. "I dreamed it, and then I heard the king order — I wanted to run ahead, to warn them, but I couldn't." Hot tears burned his eyes and his throat closed on the words.

"I learned of it when I rode back to take this road north."

It made no sense for Saman to ride north to Jerusalem when he was supposed to be avoiding King Herod, but Arash could not think.

139

"It was when you were caught listening, wasn't it?" Saman's voice was not accusatory, as Arash had expected. It was nearly gentle. That was worse.

Arash could only nod.

"He ordered you then to return with news of the child. He did not trust us to betray the new king to him."

Arash nodded again.

"But Arash, afterward you were safe with me again. Herod could not have plucked you out of our camp, even had he dared to try. Whyever did you go to him?"

"He promised...." Arash broke off in a little sob which could not begin to express his sorrow and horror. How could he say he had bartered a child's life for freedom from Saman?

Saman looked at Arash, and Arash saw he *knew*. But for the moment, he did not press. "Come on, stand up. And Ishan is trained to take two, so let's get you off those feet."

Arash could not grasp what he meant. "But...."

"I came north to find you," Saman said simply. "I've found you."

"But...."

"Come back with me, Arash," said Saman. "To Babylon first, and then on to Tyspwn. I have a great deal of research to do on the God of Belteshzzar and

Daryush, and what the prophets have to say of this new king. And I will require my drummer, and a fresh mind to ask good questions."

Arash's throat spasmed. "I've lost my drum."

Saman nodded once. "I noted. But it is simpler to replace a drum than a drummer. And I want your mind as much as your music; I said I needed your questions."

"He — he is not a king like Herod. He is not a king of the mighty."

"I believe that is true." Saman nodded. "They say he will be a savior, but I don't think it will be a salvation from the Romans or their puppet-kings. He has come for some other purpose, to save us from something greater than an empire."

Saman rose and mounted Ishan, then extended a hand to Arash. "Will you come?"

Ishan pricked his ears and looked at him. Arash swallowed and then reached up to take Saman's wrist. His master pulled him up and Arash wriggled into place behind him.

Saman turned Ishan, and they rode south to find the Megistanes and scholars and to go on to Babylon.

Thanks for reading *So To Honor Him*! Did you enjoy it? Please leave an honest review; I read every one, and I'd really appreciate it.

To learn more about my research for *So To Honor Him* or to read about my other fiction and non-fiction books, please visit:

www.LauraVanArendonkBaugh.com

You can sign up for news, sneak peeks, and pre-release specials, too!

AUTHOR'S & HISTORICAL NOTES

THIS story was inspired by the 1941 song "The Carol of the Drum," also later known as "The Little Drummer Boy." I was curious about how strongly the song has taken cultural root, even to the inclusion of drummer boy figurines in Nativity sets, and I wondered how a more historically plausible version of the carol's story might take place.

Thus began research into contemporary drums (probably a frame drum, unlike most illustrations of the carol) and the Megistanes, the priest-politicians of the Medes. It was fascinating!

Read on for historical notes and additional information on the real and fictional characters and their backgrounds.

CAO HE AND OTHERS

Not all the travelers are Megistanes of the Parthian empire; some are scholars from other lands, such as Cao He. Each name, aside from Saman and Cao He, comes from some cultural tradition of the Magi (though not from authenticated texts).

The comet observed by my fictional Cao He was indeed recorded by Chinese astrologers in 5 BC. The Silk Road was open at this time, providing trade and communication between east and west, and it is quite possible that a Han Dynasty scholar might have traveled to confer with the Megistanes. More, a tradition exists that the wise men came from China (Serica), and there is a (wholly apocryphal) second-century account of their journey. Though the manuscript is accepted as inauthentic, I wanted to honor the tradition by including Cao He.

His participation is plausible:

The discovery, unearthed in Fufeng near Xi'an, Shanxi Province, shows two carved human heads, both appearing to have a high nose and large deep-set eyes, the image of an Iranian or Caucasian. One piece also has on its headdress a mark like a cross, which has been identified as the ancient Chinese graphic sign for wu 巫. This piece was central to the study made by Victor Mair connecting Iranian magus and Chinese wu. The combination of the Western face and the Chinese word for wu shaman/magician apparently suggests that a wu shaman/magician was considered a Westerner or magus, or a Westerner thought to be a wu priest, by the Chinese people in the Central Plain. This combination agrees with the idea that the Chinese knew some religious ideas and practices related to the people from the west.

— Zhang He, "Is Shuma the Chinese Analog of Soma/Haoma?" Sino-Platonic Papers, 216 (October, 2011)

Cao He is a practitioner of early Feng Shui, known at this time as *the way of wind and water*. The south-pointing spoon is the first magnetic compass, which was developed for such divinations centuries before it was used for navigation.

THE PRIEST

The exact year of Jesus' birth has been a subject of debate for centuries (the BC-AD dating system is generally accepted as errant), and I cannot pretend to resolve the question within my little book. I've opted to set these events in 4 BC, a popular year among scholars for Christ's birth, although a reasonable argument can also be made for later.

This setting in time allowed for any of several possible high priests. I have chosen Joazar ben Boethus, as he belonged to the Boethusian sect which lived in luxury to enjoy the present, denying both afterlife and resurrection of the dead, and therefore was likely to be unimpressed by a "king" born in poverty.

THE PARTHIANS

In modern art, the Magi are nearly always depicted as three men riding camels. The source text of course gives neither their number nor their method of travel. (I've always been partial to imagining them on fine Arabian horses, myself.) But in researching I discovered the Megistanes would have been associated with the famous Parthian cavalry, from whence we still draw the phrase "Parthian shot."

When the Magus Tiridates I visited Rome in AD 66, to confirm his new kingship, he traveled with three thousand Parthian horsemen. I concluded therefore that a smaller number would not be unreasonable for a group of Magi traveling together.

THE LANGUAGE

Tyspwn is the Middle Persian name for the capital city of the Parthian empire, while *Ctesiphon* is the latinized name and more commonly seen today.

Neberu is the old Babylonian name for Jupiter.

The Greek word *tektōn* is used in scripture to describe Joseph (and later Jesus). While it has been traditionally translated "carpenter," I was tempted to use "builder" as the latter is likely more accurate, as *tektōn* may apply to both carpentry and masonry. In the end, I opted for the clarity of tradition, rather than risking confusion, but it is interesting to note that both Jesus and his adoptive father may have been trained in more than just woodworking.

While there may have been a caravansary near Bethlehem, there almost certainly wasn't an "inn" as popularly imagined. The word *kataluma* is typically translated "upper room" elsewhere in Scripture, as when Jesus ate a final meal with his disciples before his crucifixion, and refers to a house. (A commercial inn for travelers is a *pandokeion*, as used in the parable of the Good Samaritan.)

DRUMMING

Despite the story's opening comments, I did not find a strict prohibition on males playing the frame drum. There may however have been a silent cultural expectation, like many still evident in our own society, that drummers were female. I found several mentions by drum historians that most of the drummers recorded in period art are female.

> *"Depictions of smaller frame drums similar to some still used can be found in the artwork of Greece, Egypt, Persia, and India. They mainly show women playing frame drums in ritual, but men often appear in Arabic examples when a frame drum is employed for martial purposes."*
>
> *— N. Scott Robinson, "Frame Drums and Tambourines," first appearing in Continuum Encyclopedia of Popular Music of the World, Volume 2: Performance and Production, now at http://www.nscottrobinson.com/framedrum s.php.*

See also Layne Redmond's book *When the Drummers Were Women*.

GEOGRAPHY

The Midland Sea is of course the Mediterranean (Latin *mediterraneus*, "in the middle of the land" for its location between Europe, Asia, and Africa).

Tyspwn (also latinized to Ctesiphon, more commonly seen today) sat on the Tigris River in present-day Iran and was the capital of the Parthian and the Sassanid empires. It was an important city along the Silk Road, and Cao He would have stopped there en route to Babylon.

Babylon (*Bābiru*) lay between the Tigris and Euphrates Rivers and was a major city throughout much of antiquity.

THE VISIT

Where did the wise men find Jesus?

One possibility is that Jesus and his parents had returned to Nazareth by the time of the Magi's arrival. This would explain their questioning of Herod and the need to return by another route, as Bethlehem and Jerusalem are quite near geographically for the necessity of the star's reappearance and guidance. Finding Jesus in Nazareth is more consistent with the scriptural report that he was an older child rather than an infant, explains why the Magi arrived after the child's dedication at the Temple, and suggests why the whole scene wasn't just a stone's throw from Herod's palace, making his own investigation simple. Unfortunately, it makes the slaughter of the innocents even more horrific; Herod's target wasn't even in that town.

This is one place where I conceded to tradition, and I kept the family in Bethlehem at the time of the Magi's visit. It was simpler than trying to explain counter to readers' expectations without bogging down the story, and it allowed for Arash's trek between Bethlehem and Jerusalem.

But I have included the suggestion of the Nazarene visitation, so my father will be pleased.

HEROD

There is limited historical speculation that Herod drove out the residents of Qumran, the community responsible for what we know as the Dead Sea Scrolls, as the site was abandoned during his reign but occupied before and after. This involves a lot of assumption: the Qumran site is commonly held but is not proven to have been an Essene monastery, and there is no historical record of Herod's involvement with the site.

The Essenes lived strict and ascetic lives and held a messianic expectation of political deliverance, which would not have sat well with Herod's political views if indeed they were the residents of Qumran. Though it's certainly not out of character for the historical Herod as we know him, there is no historical documentation of his guilt in Qumran's abandonment; I have simply put the supposition in Saman's mouth, as a possible rumor of the time.

Though in this story Herod declares to the Magi that Antipater will inherit his throne, in historic fact he had this son executed too, shortly before his own death. His kingdom was ultimately divided among his sons Archelaus, Philip, and Antipas.

Herod died probably soon after these events, and his paranoia persisted until the very end: he intended that a number of prominent citizens should be executed upon his death, so there would be great mourning (and no rejoicing!) among his subjects. Fortunately, these orders were not carried out.

ABOUT THE AUTHOR

Laura VanArendonk Baugh was born at an early age and never looked back. She overcame her childhood deficiencies of having been born without teeth and unable to walk, and by the time she matured into a recognizable adult she had become a behavior analyst, an internationally-recognized and award-winning animal trainer, a costumer/cosplayer, a chocolate addict, and of course a writer.

Find her at:
www.LauraVanArendonkBaugh.com
She tweets at **@Laura_VAB**, too!

Other books by Laura VanArendonk Baugh:
Kitsune-Tsuki
Kitsune-Mochi
Con Job
Smoke and Fears
Fired Up, Frantic, and Freaked Out: Training Crazy Dogs from Over-the-Top to Under Control

Made in the USA
Middletown, DE
11 May 2017